Disclaimer

This is a work of fiction. Any names, businesses, characters, events, incidents and places are either the product of the author's imagination or used in a fictitious manner. Any resemblance to actual people, living or dead, or actual events or occurrences is purely coincidental.

The Sands of Time

The Angel's Blessing
Book 2

By Blaine Hart
Copyright © 2016

Check Out all My Books and Audio Books at: www.LordHartRules.com

Table of Contents

Chapter 1: Communion

My Master did not become the great warrior that he is by being soft and indecisive. While he was a man prone to thought and considering, moving slow like a master general on the battlefield, always pondering his next move, he could also be quick as a cobra when needs pressed.

But that night on the island, when we were with the Angel of Glory, I saw in Kell a slow and burning anger as the woman in the cistern's mist took the form of our beloved Anna, mocking him, and threatening the world with ninety-nine days and nights of rain, floods, and a slow but very real destruction.

She was a power that we could not know, and she did a good job of driving fear into us... at least into me, my master seemed to be immune to fear as far as I could tell.

I know that I was afraid. Her visage in the likeness of my young friend that she had abducted was a horror. Her sweetly venomous words were like a knife in my soul. Looking so much like the innocent girl, the demon's mockery goaded us and fed in me the flames of real hate, the likes of which I had never known before.

As she laughed and vanished down the Angel's cistern, I cried out in a rage and threw a knife at the fading ghostly image. The simple steel blade clattered off a wall and then fell silently into the nothingness.

"Well that was a waste," Wendfala said.

"I know," I said. "But I just – I have to –"

"You have to conserve," she said. "The power that you are facing could crush you as quick as look at you and foolish acts can come back to haunt. Curse the power, but do not give in to that power."

"It was just a knife," I said.

"So you say," Wendfala said in a stern voice, looking so much like a serious but beautiful teacher.

Wendfala was a witch and so I knew that she had charms that would make me see her as she pleased. But I did not believe that she was charming me. She was a lovely witch, all on her own. When she had saved me and my master from a watery grave, she had appeared as a mermaid. She was naked and her long locks of hair had kept her form just that side of hidden... most the time. She had kissed me below the waves and her kiss bathed me in air so that I could hold my breath as long as I wanted, and so we swam as happy as fishes all the way to the Angel's island where we had left the twins Anna and the other Anna with the

Angel Gavial. There we found the Angle's shrine in ruins, Gavial and Anna prisoners of some demonic power and the other Anna mysteriously vanished.

It was as though our great victory over the Bone Dragon had counted for almost nothing. All of our toil and stress, all of my master's cunning and magic had been just a single battle in a greater war. The realms of the Nine were safe from Visalth, the Undead Bone Dragon who my master had laid to waste, but the world was slowly being attacked by a powerful force and most didn't even know of it. They were feeling the first falling raindrops of a mighty hurricane and only we three knew just how dangerous our enemy truly was.

I could see the people of the Barnacle Atoll going about their daily lives, thinking that the spring rains were lingering. I thought about people on the fertile islands of Wan and Mirth thinking it a blessing for their fields as their low rice patties filled with the precious waters of March. None of them knew of the demon's curse, but as time passed, they would be the ones who would be overwhelmed.

After the evil thing had taunted us and bragged about her grand scheme, a very grave, almost painful look fell over my master's face. He let Ashrune slip from his fingers, the iron head thudding dully on the stone stair. As if one possessed from within, he turned and walked slowly to the shore of the cave and stared out to the gathering storm,

I looked at him standing there like a large heroic statue on the broken shell shore of the grotto. I wondered how we three, we stranded three, could ever fight such a curse against such a fearsome foe. To battle a bone dragon was one thing. Even as an undead creature it had a physical form and my master had special powers against creatures such as that. It had a head and wings and a tail that could be cut or crushed or severed. It could be faced and challenged, and defeated.

But what about the rain? Who could stop the rain? Who could conquer the clouds?

"We must see to the ship," Wendfala said.

"What?" I said shaking my head and focusing my brain.

"We must see to the repair of the ship," she said. "This place is a waste and there is nothing that we can do here. We must repair the ship so that we can go."

"Go where?" I asked.

"I don't know. But we cannot stay here. You are a sailor. Help me see to the ship."

"My master will know what to do." I said. "Kell will know."

I started walking over the crushed and crumbled gravestone to Kell standing on the shore. He stood there, looking up into the dark and stormy sky as if entranced.

"No," Wendfala said. "Leave him be. You and I should—"

"We should do nothing without my master!" I shouted.

I started to run but the woman was on me in an instant, like an owl snatching a mouse. She grabbed my arm hard but I twisted sharply and flung her off with all my strength. I dashed across the debris toward my master, but before I knew what was happening, something hit me and stopped me cold. It was as if I had run into an invisible wall. I looked up and Wendfala stood between me and my master holding out her arm. Kell still stood quietly at the shore.

"Your master," she said, "is in a state of communion. I should have thought that you would have recognized that. We ought not to disturb him. We ought to look to the ship."

"What . . .what did you do?" I said, probing the invisible force in front of me.

"I'm a witch," she said, strolling to me and taking my hand. "I can do a lot of things. Leave your master be and come with me."

The Annas small boat had been driven up and onto a place against the cave wall where the water met the rock. Its prow was well ashore and the anchor and the rest of the ship wallowed in the rolling swells of the cove. The boat bumped and rocked even as we boarded. Her mainmast was snapped and her jib lay in twisted pieces on the rocky shore. We stood surveying the wreck.

"Well?" she said. "Do you think that the two of us can repair the thing?"

"The mast will take some time," I said. "But it can be done. What worries me is that part of the prow edged onto those rocks. It looks to be stuck fast and if there is a hole, well it all depends on what kind of hole."

"It's still floating." Wendfala said in an encouraging tone.

"That's something on our side." I admitted. But the rigging is a mess."

"Are there any tools we can use?" Wendfala asked.

"Tools and some wood for repair," I said nodding. "But we will need to be very creative."

There was a double block swing at just about head height. I reached to grab for it but as I did a large wave swell rolled aft and crashed into the boat, causing me to lose my balance. I reached to break my fall and my right arm plunged into the broken mast half.

"Longo!" Wendfala screamed.

I cried out in pain. There was a four inch gouge from my wrist all the way up my arm. I clutched my arm to stem the bleeding and started cursing aloud. Wendfala grabbed my hand and sang a quick chant. My arm tingled and the blood slowed, but didn't stop. She looked at me somewhat puzzled. She clutched my hand tighter and sang her charm louder. Again there was a tingling and a sense of ease but the bleeding still trickled. Wendfala spat out a long string of cusses in a strange tongue while she looked wildly about her.

"This place," she said. "The evil of that damned demon lingers, tainting this once holy place. My powers are waning."

"There are medic supplies below," I said. "It's nothing really. I've had worse. I am sure I'll be ok. Your magic helped a good amount."

In the crew's quarters she found bandages and healing salves. The boat listed and we sat at an angle rocking gently in the grotto's low swells.

"Good news," Wendfala said as she saw to my cut. "You're going to live. Bad news; you're going to live."

"What about my master?" I asked. "What did you mean? What is a state of communion?"

"Kell is a Paladin," she said, spinning the silky gauze around my wrist. "He is holy and he has spiritual guides who watch his life and his time on this planet. I know little of these things, but I do know that when a Paladin seeks help from his guides that it is a very dangerous thing for him."

"Dangerous?" I asked. "How?"

"His very soul is vulnerable," she answered. "He casts it to the windy spheres and so meets with his mentors in a place beyond. But if the communal link would be in any way broken, for instance, by a well-meaning fool rushing up to him and shaking him, well that would be a very, very bad thing. His soul might never find his body again. The spirit winds are so fickle."

I stared at her absorbing her words.

"Back home," she said, putting the final knot on my arm dressing. "Kell could never think to seek to commune. You islanders were always popping in and out of his life. But here, here in the solitude and isolation of an Angel's shrine, where the power is at its strongest, he is seeking guidance, asking for help. I just hope the evil of this place doesn't taint his attempts."

"So," I said thinking it through. "My master's soul is meeting his own masters?"

"No," she said. "Unlike witches or wizards, a Paladin has no master. He is part of a communal whole. That's why his communion can take so long. I suspect that there is a lot of debate going on in the winds of the souls."

"Debate?" I asked. "What is there to debate? The world is in peril."

"Our world is in danger." Wendfala corrected. "There are hundreds of thousands of other worlds out there in the great whole."

I gasped. "So many? Will he be able to find a way to defeat this demon?"

"He is finding," she said. "Though I don't know what the finding will be. I do know that whatever way he discovers will not be on this island. We need to see to this battered ship and get away from this place before it becomes totally cursed."

"She's called the *Chaos*," I said, pointing at the tattered pink sails.

"Appropriate." Wendfalla chuckled. "And I do believe that she has some charms of her own," as she admired the yellow rigging.

But if the *Chaos* had any charms of healing or repair, she gave none of those up to us.

The first task was to free the ship from its rocky clutch using gaffs and poles, pushing and prying. Once she was adrift we needed to drag the skipjack ashore so that we could see the damage. We rigged blocks and tackle around stones and heaved. I was surprised at Wendfala's strength. The slender witch pulled her weight and more. We were helped by a few larger swells and I wondered about the witch's powers.

There was a buckle along the starboard prow, but the frame pieces were sound. We had to remove and replace the outer planking. The Anna's stores had some usable bits, but those weren't enough. I made pieces from the galley table. It wasn't the prettiest patch against the baby-blue hull, but it was a patch.

All the while Kell stood at the shore of the grotto looking out to sea.

The main mast had snapped like a matchstick, all splinters and fuzz. It took me three days to detach the snapped half, then cut and carve the two ends into interlocking shapes while Wendfala saw to the broken jib boom. During that time, we would both receive random injuries and be confronted with a variety of dark thoughts in our heads. It took us two more days to rig a gantry that would nestle the two halves of the mainmast together. My puzzle pieces fit and Wendfala and I joyfully hammered down the seven hoop-rings that fused the joint, then we whooped as the mast stood straight and tall in the Angel's cave. After that we rested, my arm was sore.

All the while Kell stood at the shore of the grotto looking out to sea.

"Surely he must eat," I said."

"Surely he must," Wendfala answered. "But we cannot feed him. How is your wrist?"

"Just fine," I said.

"I see that the bandages are pussing again."

"It's all this sea water." I said.

"I hope that's what it is," she said. "I hope there is no infection festering. Come, I must change them again."

"Right. After we shorten the rigging and stay the mast."

Wendfala was a worker and the work was hard. She knew what she knew and she listened to what she didn't know to do and between the two of us we had the Chaos afloat in a total of ten torturous and nightmare ridden days. We cheered and celebrated her launch when we finally pushed her back into the grotto waters.

All the while Kell stood staring out to sea with a crazy expression on his face, as if he was looking upon the ultimate glory of a God.

During those ten days my wound ached terribly. I tried to keep that from the witch, but she was no fool. She chanted her charms, but the curse of the place got stronger every day. And all this time Kell stood at the shore of the grotto. I wanted to approach him, just to see if he was alright, but Wendfala kept me away.

"He is still with his guides," she said.

While my master lingered in commune and while Wendfala and I saw to the ship, precious time passed. The demon in the Angel's well had spoken of ninety-nine days. We had already spent more than ten in the grotto. My arm felt as if it were on fire and as if tiny little demons where prodding me with little flaming tridents.

Not long after that a fever took me. Wendfala was never far from my side, only leaving to collect cool rainwater to soothe me as she sang her weakened charms. The bunk that I had taken to below in the *Chaos* became too close and warm, so Wendfala made a bed for me on deck, where sometimes a small eddy of wind would waft in through the entrance. Wendfala looked tired, haggard, and distressed. Occasionally I would still feel a vestige of the angel's holy presence about me, and in those moments I would rejoice and relish in every second of it. But they were getting scarcer and scarcer.

On the twelfth day and the second day of fever, my head began to spin terribly. I was always dizzy, even though I lay flat on my back. I began to hallucinate. Looking out into the storm outside, I started seeing lightning, not as bolts or streaks, but as weaving filaments of green and blue and gold. They whirled about as if in some sort of crazy aerial dance. They would clash together and the colors would blend and look like surreal flowers. I saw my master sometimes silhouetted, sometimes engulfed by the weird lights.

Even now, so many years later, the image of my master just sitting on the beach amidst the lightning is seared into my brain. Something I will never forget.

At the time, my body was awash in sweat and I was shivering uncontrollably. I could feel Wendfala trying to sooth my brow with cool wet rags, but in my state, it was as though they burned.

In my crazy delirium I would pray for just a hint of the angel's presence, just a few seconds of reprieve. Then I thought that I heard singing. The singing of more than a dozen voices, each one miles away. The singing became louder and they began to croon in a lovely sweet harmony. I thought they might be divine angels come to save me, and in that thinking I felt a wave of serenity wash over me, body and soul. I closed my eyes and saw the angel of glory once again.

I then opened my eyes and something hovered over my head like a bright halo. It was circling my head and transmitting a bright light all around me, and especially onto my injured arm. Then the bright halo exploded into a thousand pieces. When my vision cleared, it was as if a void had been left in the darkness. In that void I saw a vision of a polished marble tombstone with its back to me. As I gazed, it began to slowly turn. I half expected to see my name carved on it, but what I saw was puzzling.

There was a round silver medallion set into the white stone. It was the shape of a most curious looking tree. Branches and roots sprung from the trunk, but the branches and roots were like a mirror of each other. The upper branches flowed into a knot-like network of leaves that traced around the circle and down into the roots, forming another mesh of delicate weavings. On the top and on either side of the twining leaves were strange runes that had been carved. Something in me yearned to have the thing and I reached for it –

And then I began to feel as if something was welling inside of me. As if my soul was gathering in the strength of the universe, there was a stirring, and that sense of ease and calm told me that all would be well. In that peaceful moment I had a small longing to see my master and Wendfala just one more time. I so wanted to say—

"Goodbye," I said. sitting bolt upright.

Then there was laughter.

"I think you mean 'hello'," Kell said.

"Master!"

"How are you feeling?" he asked.

"I – I feel," I began, but then I was puzzled.

My fever was gone. The fire in my arm was quenched. I was covered in sweat and grime, but I felt sound and whole as I looked up into my master's smiling face.

"I feel great!"

Chapter 2: Selivanova

"Paladin, your blessing is strong," Wendfala said. "You healed the boy when I could not."

Indeed, I was healed. I sat up and looked about as if I had just woken from a pleasant nap. I was slightly confused and feeling groggy, but it was as though nothing had happened. Wendfala began un-wrapping the bandage from my arm, and when she had, she sat back and smiled. My wrist looked as if there had never been a wound. There wasn't even a scar.

"It must be a mighty blessing," she said. "The green-death had set in and I was afraid that I was going to have to remove the arm. And now – and now he is whole. It is a mighty blessing indeed."

"A blessing is not the word," Kell said. "My guides are not deities. It is the Strength of my Ancestors. The Paladins who have gone before me and who are now my guides have granted me much. But unlike a blessing, the Strengths come at a cost, and there will be a reckoning."

"A reckoning?" she said. "Why would your Ancestors make you pay for something that will help the world?"

"Because they care little for our world. All that we see, the Nine Realms and beyond are but little in the Cosmos that they inhabit. But they did not make me pay; I was the one who made the offer."

I saw that Wendfala was about to ask what he offered, but Kell held up his hand and stopped her. I stared a moment at that hand, and to me it looked as though it had hints of the weird and wonderful colors of the strange lightning I had seen in my delirium.

"But I see that you have not been idle," he said. "The *Chaos* looks fit to sail, and so sail we must."

"And so she shall sail," Wendfala said. "Young Longo here is a bright and clever shipwright and teacher too. I have learned much as well and I will help as we sail. But only if that sailing is to lead us to stopping the she-devil in the well and breaking her spell of rain."

"It is as you say and how it must be." Kell said gravely, his eyes turning to steel.

"Then where do we go now master?" I asked.

"To the Island where the Tree of Life resides," he said, "to Seek the Blessing from the Angel of Life."

"B-but no one can go there," Wendfala said. "No mortal has ever set foot on that sacred soil. It is said that the island is an earthly portal to Iteatu."

"The Angelic Meadows." I said.

"No mortal has set foot... yet." Kell said. "That does not mean that no mortal can. We have to try. Only with a blessing of Life can we begin to think about challenging the demon witch Moanmalla."

"Moanmalla?" I said. "Is that her name?"

Kell nodded. Wendfala turned ashen.

"How do we get there?" I asked. "How do we get to these sacred groves?"

"I don't know," Kell said.

We were suddenly a strange lot. We had a ship, we had a task, we had a crew, but we didn't know where to go. We could sail, and with Wendfala's magic, we knew that we could weather most any storm, but without a direction, we would simply blindly trust the winds.

Kell and Wendfala talked long. They spoke of legends and myths and stories that they had heard and of those I knew little of. I felt useless, and so I did what I always do when I am frustrated; I went below deck and I began to cook.

The Annas had stored away a goodly provision of dried meats and vegetables. I boiled a pot of rainwater and began a soupy-stew. The shriveled caulibroks looked like little trees. I sliced off the withered bases and tossed them into the pot with a bit of oil. They took to the water like thirsty rabbits and they swelled quickly. As I stirred in the meat, the water began to steam and the caulibroks floating on top bumped and bustled in odd ways. I watched inhaling the aroma.

Two florets swirled and knocked as if they were in a dance. It was both amusing and compelling, then a bit of a blob of oil surrounded them began swelling and making a perfect circle. The caulibroks rolled in that circle, bouncing off of their swelling flowers. Then they whirled until their bases touched, and in that touch they clung together. I stared. The vision from my delirium came back and I saw the tree on the tombstone as clear as if Gavial herself had shown it to me.

I left my cooking and dashed topside. I jumped from the ship and splashed to the shattered shore.

"Longo!" Wendfala cried. "Longo what are you doing?"

"Searching," I called back. "Searching for a tombstone. It's here. It's here among the fallen."

"What -- what are you talking about?"

"Just – just help me. Please."

I splashed ashore and started groping in the dark, feeling the fallen tombstones and trying to find the white marble one. Kell and the witch anchored the ship and then Kell splashed into the ocean and swam to follow me. Wendfala stood behind, muttering and waving her hands.

"What are you looking for?" Kell asked when he had finally caught up. "And why are you so frantic?"

"I saw something," I said as I searched. "In my fever, I saw your hand and then I saw a tombstone, and on that tombstone was—"

The area suddenly lit. Kell had Ashrune raised to the sky and it glowed with the light of the sun. But I had no eyes for the magic. I frantically searched for white marble. There were many cracked, broken or shattered tombstones. I soon found one that lay almost whole. I scurried to it. It had a blank back. I dug and pulled with all my strength, but it wouldn't budge.

Then my master stood over while Wendfala floated to the ground next to me and pulled me away. Kell was smiling.

"Gavial," he said so softly. "You are a wonder."

He lowered the head of Ashrune and the light bathed the marble. Then he muttered strange words and the stone began to tremble. It rose, and as it did I could hear the rocks and debris around it shift and tear. Then it pulled from the earth, levitated a moment, and then slowly rotated until the face was clear to see.

On that face I saw the medallion of my vision.

Then Kell laughed aloud and the slab fell with a crash and shattered, leaving the silver medallion sparking under my master's holy light. I reached down and took up the silver medallion. It was warm and one of the runes on its side seemed to glow ever so faintly. My hand trembled.

"Gavial has blessed you Longo." my master said. "From her bondage she reached into your fevered soul. Thank her."

"But what is it?" I asked.

"It is our loadstone," he said. "It is the compass that will point the way to the Sacred Island. You have been blessed."

We swam back to the ship while Wendfala floated next to us. There was no wind so we had to row the ship across the grotto, and as Kell and I took to the oars, I found my strength was suddenly far stronger than it ever had been. My back, legs and arms felt as if I could row us all the way back to the Barnacle Atoll. I looked to my master and he smiled but said nothing. We said farewell to Gavial's grotto and headed into the rolling sea.

A few hours later nature's winds caught us full, the sails snapped and we were speeding on our way. The question was which way? Wendfala sang a small charm that sheltered me from the winds and I took out the Angel's loadstone. I dangled it on some rope and we watched the talisman slowly turn back and forth until it settled a few points off the port bow. The rune glowed and there it stayed fixated. We looked to the sky, and while the rain was constant it was day and we saw the faintest image of the bright sun behind the clouds. Kell took the wheel and steered until the ship was on a line with the loadstone. We had something of a bearing and so we sailed.

The swells were fickle, one moment they would be long smooth rollers and the next they would crest like small hills that the boat would mount on a steep angle, only to have the prow go slapping down onto the waters on the other side. None of us were strangers to the sea, but the work was taxing. The helm was hard to manage, for the waves and wind were rolling one way, while we were headed another way all the while a deep and swift current from below was going a third direction. But even during my time at the wheel, wrestling to stay on our line, it felt as if my muscles had been charmed and I fought the thing with what felt like the strength of two men. I wondered if my master's healing had given me more than health.

So on our voyage went. Our time was divided between the wheel, the rigging, and sleep. Two of us were always on deck. Twice a day we would check the loadstone and correct our course. The skies were a constant gloom and the rain sometimes came in waves and torrents. After three days we could tell that it was night, only because the darkness was deeper. We were drenched to the bone and miserable. The ships pitching and plowing made any sort of fire in the galley impossible and so we ate cold boards. There wasn't even any good hot tea.

On our fourth day at sea the waters seemed to calm even though the rain held steady. Without sun or stars to plot our course, Kell could only guess where we were, and he guessed us to be in the Junes Straights, a long stretch of water between the continents of Fesul to the west and Dobrul to the east. Our drinking water was running low and we did not trust the demon rain, so we were on watch for land. As the waters quieted more and more, Wendfala stood over a small fire in the stove. We finally had time for some delicious tea.

The morning of the fifth day was my watch on the ratlines. Here the sun managed to brighten the clouds some, and though the rain made visibility poor, it was better than seeing dark mountainous swells. I was peering to the east, thinking that I had seen some shadowy form, when someone called my name.

"What?" I called back.

Kell looked up to me puzzled.

"What?" he said.

"Didn't you call me?"

"No." he said in a gruff voice.

I shrugged it off and returned to searching the horizon for what I could see. Then someone called me again, and the sound was as clear as day. Wendfala had just come on deck.

"Did you call me Wendfala?"

She looked at me and shook her head.

"Though it is your time to rest," she said. "I'll take the watch."

"And rest you should," Kell said. "You're hearing things."

Too much time spent on a single mind numbing task could do that. I began to climb down when I heard my name again.

"Longo."

It sounded somewhat distant and yet so very sweet, and I knew that it could not have been either of my crew mates. I'd have sworn that it had come from the water. I looked about. The rain ws splashing on the sea and the sound was constant. Then I thought I saw a small splash, as if something had dove into the water. I scanned the area even as Wendfala called for me to come down. But I was entranced. I had to see what was there... and then I saw something red break the surface of the ocean.

There was gleaming green hair, and then a beautiful face looked up at me. She had the soft, round innocent eyes of a child and yet her face was mature like a woman. She seemed to propel herself almost all the way out of the water, and her streaming, gleaming hair flowed all down her comely body.

"Longo," she said softly, reaching her arms to me.

Something in me stirred. Her eyes were so sad and it was as if just in looking at her my heart was breaking. In that moment I was overwhelmed with a desire to hold her and to comfort her. But even as I reached over the ship deck for her, she slid back away from me into the water, her silken green hair swirling behind.

"Longo come down!" Kell cried.

"Did you see –"

"I saw," Kell said. "It is a Rusalka. Look away and come down now!"

But even as he spoke, I saw the waters swell and the beautiful child-woman rose up again, but this time even higher. Her streaming hair trailed a line of white water and she floated up so that she could look me in the eyes while revealing beautifully perfect breasts. She lovingly called my name and reached a delicate hand to me.

"Longo!" Kell shouted. "Don't touch her!"

But I was driven by an overwhelming urge in my soul, and I stretched my hand toward her. Just as I was about to clasp her hand, I cried out in pain as a belaying pin knocked it away. I lost my balance and flailed in the rigging. I caught myself and turned in time to see her glowing green hair flow back below the waves. I clutched the lines and ignored hand the pain in my hand.

I was barely aware of Kell calling me. I prepared to jump into the ocean to save the beautiful damsel, but the next thing I knew Wendfala had pushed me further into the lines, her body tangled with mine. I heard the water part and strained to look at the ocean. I turned my head and there was the nymph again, stretching for me, her eyes looking so pained and my soul aching to comfort her.

"No!" Wendfala cried. "You cannot have him!" she screamed. Her hand then glowed brightly and she slapped me viciously across the face.

She then turned towards the woman and green fire flew from her fingers. The thing in the water screamed and instantly disappeared underneath the water. I was overcome with rage, and right there in the lines, I let go and cuffed her in the face. She grunted and her nose bled badly, maybe even broken. I was like a demon possessed. I grabbed her throat and began to throttle her. She punched me in the gut and kneed me between the legs. I groaned and crumbled. She caught me by the scruff of my collar and brought me to the deck before Kell.

More water nymphs were rising from the sea all about us, moaning and wailing and calling my name, pleading and imploring me.

"Longo," one wept. "The witch has hurt Selivanova."

"You must help her," another wailed.

"She is dying."

"Save her."

"Save her Longo."

The rage rekindled in my heart and I felt as if I were on fire. My green haired woman was not among the bobbing fairies and I was in a weird agony. I had to see her again. Ignoring my pains I scrambled to my feet but Wendfala was before me. I drew my dagger, yelled like a berserker and lunged at her , but even as I did she waved her arms and I slumped to the deck and rolled as one paralyzed. Then the witch turned to the creatures, but Kell stayed her.

"No," he said. "We must not harm them."

"But there are so many of them," she cried. "They could overwhelm us."

"No. They are Rusalka. They cannot leave the waters where they were murdered."

"Murdered?"

"Horribly," one of them moaned. "Violated and cast away to drown while still in the flower of youth."

"We only seek some small peace."

"Give us the boy. Please."

"His tender soul will comfort us."

"For a small while," Kell said. "I grieve for your lonely and painful doom, but you cannot have the lad. Leave us and seek your tranquility elsewhere as your bodies go to their natural fate. Now Go." Kell bellowed, raising Ashrune above his head and muttering a holy chant underneath his breath.

"Nooooo," they wailed.

For hours they followed the ship, rising from the waters and calling out their sorrowful pleas. Kell and Wendfala carried me below. I was still under her spell of holding and while I could no longer see the water spirits, their moans haunted my soul. Wendfala cradled and soothed me as a mother, all the while keeping me motionless.

"I pity you my friend," Kell said, placing his hand on my heart. "You touched Selivanova, and so her sorrow will haunt you the rest of your days. I can see to your harms but I cannot mend your heart. You must be strong."

His healing flowed through me like a wellspring of serenity. Wendfala let go her spell and I held her tight and cried like a child the whole time.

"Think of the Angel," she said soothingly.

Chapter 3: Evil Waters

Our seventh day at sea we hailed a vessel and followed her to a port where the people were surprised to see such a small craft so far from home. But they were kind, and when Kell told them that he was Holy Paladin, they gave us all the fresh well water and food that we could carry in exchange for some of his healing. We lingered a day among these people to recuperate and dry our bones, and I relished standing on ground that did not rock and sway.

The people implored Kell to do something about the incessant rains, but he said that it was beyond his power. As we took back to sea with the next morning's tide, I asked my master why we hadn't told the people of Moanmalla's curse. He shook his head.

"Demons are selfish," he explained. "If they ask you to do something then it will always be for their own good. Were we to do as she bade us, then fear would spread in the world and she would draw strength from that. Better that people have some hope that the rains will end than be afraid for the end of days."

The next day we sailed. Guided by our silver loadstone necklace, we kept a southerly course. The waters and the weather warmed, but the rains never ceased. The air itself became damp and breathing was sometimes a chore. The winds calmed and the waters rolled in long swells. Here the cloud cover was thinner and sunlight lit them up a dull grey, but always there was rain.

We found some amusement in those balmy waters. For a while we were chased by a family of sharkodils. They playfully swam and leapt and rolled all about us, sometimes calling to us with their high whiney yelps. After a time, they became bored with our little boat and vanished. We spotted a pod of huge crimson threshers schooling east. We watched two come full surface and blow their spume in tall geysers, much to my delight.

On the second morning from our landfall, we saw something curious in the far distance. There was light. To me it looked like the moon creeping up the horizon swathed by clouds. Kell smiled.

"The Island of the Tree of Life," he said softly. "It has to be."

Then Wendfala put words to all our secret fears.

"If it is not," she said. "I believe that our quest is doomed. I count us twenty-two days since the wretched rains began and the demons curse will only grow stronger. If we have spent all this time chasing nothing, I cannot imagine what we will do."

Kell said nothing.

The light seemed so far off. The air calmed and began to stifle us with the humidity. In time we had to rely on the witch's spells. She conjured a fair wind, but doing so was a strain on the woman and so she rested often. We moved in starts and stops and so Kell and I took to the oars often. That was when I began to see the strangest creatures popping up from the water.

At first I was afraid for they seemed to have dark human hair and I thought them to be more murdered souls. Then one leapt full out of the water and I was amazed. At first I thought it was an otter. It was small like those cute little sea animals. It had four feet and a small flat face.

The thing jumped and landed on my oar, and then I saw it was no otter. It had beady dark eyes surrounded by red orbits. It had no fur but for the hair on its head draping down its skinny body. Its four legs were bent like a dog's but it had paws, all with pointed claws like a lizard. It clutched the oar shaft and stared at me. Then it bared terrible pointed fangs and hissed at me. Instinctively I recoiled and snapped the oar and flung it off. Then I heard Wendfala scream from the wheel.

I leapt to my feet and saw Kell fling one of the things from her shoulders. I felt something land on my back, and then – and then strange things began to happen.

It was as though I was moving on thought. Quick as lightening I flung off my vest and the creature went sailing. Another leapt at me and I batted the thing away with my oar. One of them landed on the rigging. I heard its hiss and only managed to jump out of its way in the nick of time. It thumped on the deck and I kicked it overboard.

I backed quickly away from the edge but the creatures were suddenly everywhere. I heard Wendfala shriek out a war cry and a dozen of them burst into flame. The three of us were backing our way to the mast. Kell and I were using our oars like mace's while Wendfala was casting her magic frantically.

"They're like a swarm," she cried.

They were all over the ship and coming at us from the water and from the rigging. We should have been overwhelmed but we three were fighting and slaying like warriors charged with lightning. My reflexes were instant and my aim was always true. Soon my swing was taking out two or three at a time, but always they came."

"Is there no end to them?" I yelled.

"They'll overpower us with sheer numbers," Wendfala wailed between spells.

My master got angry. He gave a roar that seemed to shatter the sky and a dozen of the creatures were blasted from the lines and into the ocean. He gave another cry and Ashrune flew into his hands. Then he became like a madman, his war hammer blurring and blazing through the air so that I could only hear the sounds of their bones shattering. Then it was as if I had caught my master's insanity and my oar slashed through the ugly creatures with blazing speed.

As we fought and slashed the vermin, the ship shuddered and suddenly it was as if the *Chaos* was lifted. The sails furled and billowed and we were propelled across the water faster than an eagle-fish. As we sped through the water the attacks slowed, but those that did assault us were still vicious. My master and I wiped them from sky, sea and deck.

In time they were gone. We could hear their frustrated leaping and splashing from far away. Kell and I stayed our weapons. We breathed. We looked about. The deck was littered with their corpses and slimed with their vile blood. I had several bites and claw marks on my body, but nothing too bad. The wind eased. Then I heard a groan and I just managed to catch Wendfala as she collapsed.

"She saved us," Kell said. "She used her magic to conjure a mighty wind. But now she is paying the price. She is exhausted, drained."

"Will she be alright?" I asked, not knowing if I should be afraid.

"I don't know," he said, gathering her limp frame in his arms. "It will take much for her to recover. Her harms are not so much physical as spiritual, and there my healing can reach only so far."

"But . . . but she will be alright," I said as if begging. "Please say that she will."

"If she can last the night," Kell said. "I will make her comfortable and do what I can. You, Longo, must see to these wicked corpses. This ship must be cleansed of their evil before night falls."

"What are these things?"

"They are Dobhar-chu," he said. "Creatures created by a dark sorcerer. He has long since passed but these things have bred and outlived his schemes. Be thorough in your work lad, Wendfala's life will depend on it."

I puzzled on his words as I tossed the creatures overboard. One still had some life in it and snapped at me. I was again amazed at the speed with which I avoided those fangs and throttled the life out of him. Something had happened to me and I knew that I had to ask my master about it later.

Dark was growing and a cool seemed to be creeping in with it. I swabbed the deck, determined to wash away every speck of the Dobhar-chu's stinking blood. There was a soft wind in the sail and I looked to the tiller now and again. As night came on, the glow before us in the south seemed somewhat brighter. There was no more need for the lodestone and so I kept the ship pointed true. As night gathered, Kell came topside with a tall cup of strong tea for me. He stood by my side and looked to the distant glow.

"There is dark magic in these waters," he said. "And that magic wants Wendfala's soul. There will be a battle tonight."

"I am ready master," I said. "Just tell me what to do."

"You must not sleep," he said. "You must look to the ship and keep our course. Other than that you can do nothing. I am going to stand watch. Do not speak to me, do not cry out and do not make a sound. No matter what you see and no matter what you hear, just look to the ship."

"But master—"

He cut me off with his hand and walked to the prow where he sat as if in vigil. There was an eerie quiet about. There were no sounds of birds, no splashing of fish, no sloshing of waves and not even the sound of wind. Only the eternal rain pelting the sea and the occasional creek of the mast broke the silence. With the night cold came a fog and the glow from the island was obscured. I still had the mark on the binnacle with which to guide the *Chaos,* and so I obeyed my master and looked to the ship.

As the night crept on I began to be afraid. I didn't know what I feared. In truth it must have been the fear of the unknown. Kell had said that there would be a battle, but I saw nothing in the night.

A few hours into that lonely watch the wind began to pick up. It was a cold wind. The sea beneath me began to pitch and roll and we were still enshrouded in the fog. I thought that I heard a low moaning in the wind.

Suddenly the hatch burst open and then just as suddenly it slammed closed. I stared in amazement as the hatch seemed to be wrestled back and forth by invisible forces. I thought to slam in the locking bar, but I didn't know if it was better for it to be open or shut. Kell had said to do nothing, so I tended the wheel in the heavy wind. A few moments later the banging had ceased and the hatch lay closed and sat quiet.

I kept thinking that I saw things; things that when I looked at them weren't there. They were like a small strike of blue or purple light that melted like the vapor trail of a falling star. They seemed to be all about, but always when I looked closely they were gone.

The wind began to swirl. The sails were flopping every which way and the ship began to yaw so I ran and trimmed the sheets. We steadied, but then we began to list a little to starboard. We had taken on no water, so I dashed back to the wheel and it had turned off course several points. I tried to right the thing, but it was like trying to shove the rudder through mud. I strained and finally managed to get the ship on course, but we were still leaning.

Then I saw that we were moving faster. The needle in the binnacle was going crazy, pointing more and more to port and way off our course. That was when I realized that were sailing in a sweeping arc, and despite all my efforts with the wheel, we were going around in a wide circle. The water was sliding fast beneath us and I knew that we had been caught in a strong current or eddy. All I could do was try and keep the ship upright. All the while Kell sat motionless in the prow.

The wind was howling and behind those howls I heard faint shrieks. There were bumps and thuds from below and I wanted to rush down there, but my master's last words stayed me. We were moving faster and listing sharper. We were in a whirlpool and I thought that the evil assaulting us was dark enough to kill us all to get Wendfala's soul. I could not see the eye of the whirlpool due to the dark and fog, but the ship was gaining speed.

Many times since I had left the peace and serenity of the Barnacle Atoll I had faced death and lived to tell the tale. But here I truly despaired. I was in the hands of evil forces powering the elements themselves and there was not a thing that I could do about it. No sword, no knife, no weapon that I could lay my hands on would have changed a thing. I was in the grip of the invisible and my fate lay in the strength of my master battling the spirits.

I was gripped by the thought of what it would be like to drown when I heard the strangest of noises. At first I thought that a flock of gulls had also been swept up in the elemental surges. I heard the flapping of a thousand wings and looked up – but there was nothing there other than the noise of shrieking and cawing –

Cawing!

I strained to see. A blitz of dark birds was flying against the wind and in the midst of the gaggle I saw a fleck of white. Round and round they flew and they seemed to calm the wind. A thousand birds were charging and flying against the unnatural force. Their cawing came from their little souls and it was music to my ears as they beat back the winds with their magic. I felt that the ship was slowing, ever so slightly. But it was slowing.

Then Kell suddenly burst to his feet. He was bathed in a glorious white light.   He held his warhammer Ashrune high in the air, and the light that enveloped him flew upward and into storm. In the burst of blinding light I saw the myriad of black crows, and then I saw Byrinius, and my heart soared. I heard unnatural shrieking in the wind and Ashrune's light ate away at the fog and the dark.

The ship's wheel spun before me as the *Chaos* righted itself. I grappled with the thing and finally wrested control. The crows cawed repeatedly as if in celebration. When I looked up again, the brilliance of my master's magic had eaten away the darkness as water will eat away at the walls of a castle made of sand. There was one last burst of white light and then it was dark once again.

The night had returned.

The water calmed. The air was still. Kell slowly lowered his war hammer. The giant white bird alit on the deck by the closed hatch, and in a twinkling Byrinius stood there. That was when I knew that it was over.

But there was something odd in the now silent night. It was not just quiet, it was too silent. There was no rain. I looked up and I saw the stars.

That quiet night my master and I slept on the deck while Byrinius went below to be with Wendfala. Kell and I woke the next morning to a real sunrise on placid water. We also woke to the smell of good tea and a delicious breakfast that Wendfala served to us. She kissed Kell and I both on the forehead and sang a small chant. I did not know what charm she had laid on us, but I do remember feeling invigorated.

"Thank you," she said softly. "You saved my very soul. You called my rooks Kell, and you Longo stayed the ship. You saved me."

"You saved our very lives," Kell said. "That was no sailors wind that you raised. It was a true gale and it got us from those little devils fast."

"I wonder," I said as I munched, "why the Dobhar-chu didn't follow. Surely those fish-like nasties could have caught up to us in time."

"It's because they are fish," Kell said. "They are spawned from a horrible cross-breeding, but at heart they are fish, and fish have very small brains. They breached and dove in their rage and after a while forgot what their rage was about and so went on seeking other prey."

"But what was the evil that sought Wendfala?"

"The same evil that spawned the Dobhar-chu," the witch said. "Evil swims with evil. It lurks deep in the waters and sensed my weakened spirit."

"There should be buoys," I said, "to warn sailors."

"No doubt there are," Wendfala said. "We must have missed them in the darkness."

"And now we are in light," I said. "And while I don't think that Moanmalla's cursed has lifted, I do suspect that we are close to the Island of the Tree of Life."

"Indeed," Kell said, inhaling the fresh sea scented air. "And if nothing else, I am glad for the relief from that maddening rain."

I too was glad. I let the sunshine warm me and thought about simple blessings. For indeed, as I looked about, it was as if we were in the eye of a hurricane, circled by dark churning clouds and storms that where just a few miles away. Those dark clouds reminded me of the true weight of our quest and how we had just barely begun. Kell too looked about.

"There's no wind," he said. "You know what that means Longo."

"To the oars we go," I said cheerily. "I feel as though I could row to – that reminds me master, I wanted to ask. When we were battling the little Dobies, it felt as if I was possessed by a spirit of strength and – and agility. I felt as if I were moving like a master elf swordsman; each of my blows was straight and true and it was as if I could anticipate their attacks."

"I too sensed that," Wendfala said. "Did you bless us Kell?"

"In a sense," he said. "The strength that the Paladin Ancestors bestowed on me is getting stronger. Those who are in my reach and in my heart share in my physical blessing."

"Is it temporary like the Angel of glory's blessing?" I asked. "How long will it last?"

"As long as I live and you are in my reach and in my heart." He responded, giving me a bright smile.

"Master," I said with a laugh. "Together we could win the annual tournaments quite easily."

"We need to stop the curse and get back to the tourneys first," he chuckled. "Let's grab some oars."

"First," I said, "help me raise the sails."

"But there's no wind."

"The canvas has been soaked for weeks," I said. "They're going to mold and then rot. Magic is a good and helpful thing, but it is no substitute for good stewardship."

"Longo is quickly becoming master of this boat," Wendfala said with a smile.

"It's a ship," I said.

We raised the canvas and I could see it drinking in the sun. Then Kell and I happily set to the oars, and that became a game between him and me as we vied to see who could pull the longest and most propelling stroke. The island came closer and closer and the work was a delight as the *Chaos* sliced through still waters. The air was fresh and the sun was on our faces. We had a task and there was no magic or scheming. There were just two men in good work with Wendfala cheering them along.

The sacred island neared. It looked like a tangle of glistening green foliage. As we approached, we looked for a shore or someplace to anchor. But everywhere around us the greenery was growing from the water, making a spindly green wall that attached to the island shore and high into the sky. I wondered what kind of plant would grow from seawater.

We slowed as we closed in. We banked and turned so that we rowed with the sun behind us and the island on my side. We were so close that we could almost touch the gleaming vines and broad diamond shaped leaves reaching high above us. Below us the crystal clear water plunged to dark depths, and so there would be no anchorage. "We should just grapple a vine and climb on." I said, but Kell kept us rowing. The vines and leaves crept by as we continued rowing for what seemed like an hour.

"There," Kell said, pointing ahead.

I saw a beach. It was a pretty white sand beach and I thought that I saw something small and alive on it going between the water to the shore. We rowed. As we came closer to the white stands, I saw a little boy. He was dressed in worn britches as if he were a castaway. He had a small bucket and was running back and forth between sand and land.

"Hello!" I called waving.

The boy stopped and stared as the *Chaos* came ashore. He was like a cherub without wings. His face was innocent and he looked on us with genuine wonder. His downy yellow hair fluttered in the breeze and his round blue eyes were both beautiful and compelling. Behind him was a small simple crude sand castle and he looked like a delicate ragamuffin out on a special holiday.

"Who are you?" he said in a soft voice.

"My name is Longo." I said as I jumped onto the shore, followed closely by Kell and Wendfala.

"You're ugly." The little boy said.

"And you are not," I said. "Are you an Angel?"

"You're stupid too."

And so saying he turned his back, dropped his little pail. and vanished in a sparkle of glittering light.

Chapter 4: Cheaters

"I suppose that I am ugly," I said to my master as we anchored the *Chaos*. "It's been a while since I've had a proper bath and a shave."

"We are all a motley crew," he said. "I hope the Angel doesn't take offence."

"Do you think that the child was the Angel in disguise?"

"No," he said. "As it was with Gavial. the Angel will have a guardian."

"A child?"

"Haven't you yet learned to not be deceived by looks?"

Byrinius came flying out of the sky and joined us in his human form, his black skin a stark contrast to the white sandy beach. The shore had a very strange shape. A round spit of sand jut into the calm waters and it seemed that the waves lapping at the shore did not wear away any of its perfect shape. A few feet in there was a long stretch of pristine white sand bordered on three sides by the oddest vegetation that I had ever seen. To our right, the plants were lush and green. There were tendrils like gleaming green vines and from them sprouted a tangle of tear shaped fronds of the same color. To our left was all brown. It was not as if they were dead, but rather they were like woody creepers. They too were thick sprouting with fine hairs all over them weaving and twisting together. Where the brown met the green in the middle of the white sand rectangle, the two seamlessly merged and their colors blended. Wendfala and I walked to the vines while Kell and Byrinius examined the wood.

It was all a tangle that reached well over our heads. The stalks and stems intertwined, blocking out most of the sun when we tried to look through them. Wendfala and I made our way along the dense growth and saw no break or path. I wondered if we should not get some machetes from the ship and hack our way inland, but then I doubted if my master would even consider harming any living thing on the island of the Sacred Tree of Life. We met Kell and Byrinius where the two plants merged.

"There is no way into the island where we searched, "Byrinius said. "Any luck on that side?"

Wendfala and I shook our heads.

"Perhaps," Wendfala said, "that there's clearer ways someplace else on the island."

Kell was frowning, staring at something. I followed his gaze to a place where tiny brown hairs meshed with tender light green shoots. He reached out to touch them but stopped. He stood back.

"Wendfala," he said, "give a wind, just a light breeze will do."

We gave her space and she waved her arms and sang her charms and the air began to flutter. In a moment it became a small wind and the tiny brown and green tendrils began to stir, then they separated like entwined fingers opening up and in a moment there was a small archway that led into the island. Kell smiled.

Inside and there was an alcove of the plants. On both sides were tunnels through the foliage that went straight a little ways and then turned. To our left on the woody side it smelled of earth and musk and the sunlight filtered through. To our right the plant side smelled so fresh and clean, but the light was dim.

"Anyone have a coin?" Kell said.

"I say left," Wendfala said. "We should walk with the light."

"I say right," Byrinius said. "I have spent my life darting about the gloom of trees and I need a little light."

"I say," I began, "that we split up—"

"No." they said together.

We decided to trust Byrinius and his bird instincts. So with a stern warning from Kell to do no harm to the plants, we plunged in single file, Byrinius leading the way. The air was close and humid, but the scent was light and pleasing. Small shafts of light filtered through and it was like walking in green shadows.

We had not gone a hundred steps past the first curve when we were confronted with a choice; two ways diverged before us. We took the left path, but all too soon we were confronted with another two choices of ways to go, and we quickly realized that the plant tunnels were a maze. Byrinius led us, alternating between left and right, reasoning that it might lead us inland. And for a few moments we thought that idea would work. The air became fresher and then we saw light ahead. We cheerfully ran to that light. Then we stopped defeated. We were right back at the entrance alcove.

I resisted any comments about bird-brains.

We tried twice again, through the green ways, and our third attempt heartened us for we had walked longer than either of our other attempts. But in the end, all that we accomplished was a long brisk walk back to where we started.

Then Wendfala, undaunted, took the lead and we plunged into the woody section. But again our efforts were futile and after the second try we flopped back on the beach sand. "It could be just one bad choice at the crucial intersection that is throwing us off." I said.

I went back to the *Chaos* for some food and drink. I left my companions discussing things and when I returned, Byrinius was gone. Kell and Wendfala were looking to the sky where a white rook soared.

"Aerial surveillance," I said. handing out bread and cheese. "Should have thought of that first."

"It's a last resort," Wendfala said. "Byrinius cannot change his form as easy as you change your socks. This transformation will be the last in a while. When he returns it will be as a crow and it will be difficult for him to communicate what he has seen."

"But he's your familiar," I said. "Can't you talk to him?"

"He is my familiar in things spiritual. As a human can he understand our concepts, but his times as a man is fleeting and far between. He cannot comprehend things mundane in his true form."

Again I bit my tongue about bird-brains.

The sun was warm, I was filthy and grimy, the rippling sea looked ever so inviting and I so wanted to swim. Kell thought that a splendid idea and as we stripped down I realized that I still wore the loadstone medallion. Wendfala needed to wait for Byrinius and so I gave the thing to her for safe keeping.

The water was mild and so relaxing. I could feel the dirt of days sliding off of me. My master and I swam and floated and floated and swam. It was so good having just a small time of delight and relaxation. The sun was just past its noon as we relaxed, almost dozing on our backs. I don't know how long it was before we heard the cawing of the white rook. We immediately swam back to shore. The bird was perched on Wendfala's arm and the two were gazing eye to eye.

"This island is a circle," she said, never breaking her stare. "There are places like . . . like this one. Places where the sand meets the trees and wood."

The crow bobbed its head three times.

"Three such places . . . no four. This place and three others. They are different, they look like . . . like man-scratch – I don't understand. They are . . . they are, I'm not sure what he's trying to tell me, they are against each other – no, they are away from each other . . . I can't—"

"They are opposite," I said.

In her other hand she still held my medallion. I saw the runes; man scratches opposite.

"Wendfala," I said. "Show him the loadstone."

She held the thing to him. He stared a moment, then two. His head flicked rapidly side to side. Then he spread his wings and let out a triumphal cry. He pecked at the thing on one of the runes and called out again.

Wendfala smiled and cooed to him. He calmed. The two reached to touch beak to lips and then he flew away out over the sea.

"Your medallion," Wendfala smiled, "is also a map."

The three of us stared down at it. It was so simple. The greenery was the branches and leaves and the woody stuff were the roots. The spit of land on which we landed was in the shape of the rune *Thyn*. We studied, searching for some sort of clue through the maze. The tangling of branches and roots was like a Celtic knot, but as any sailor will tell you, all knots can be undone.

"I found it," I said.

I traced my finger along a path that wove along the branches, and then down from the upper center in a twisting path, that ultimately led to a limb that led to the trunk and the heart of the island. It stood out to me as plain as if someone were drawing it with some magic pencil.

"Well done," Kell said. "Well done Longo the cunning."

We wasted no time. My master and I dressed and we three plunged into the maze. I led slowly and cautiously. I did take some wrong turns, but with my companions help and encouragement, we pressed on. For the longest time it was like walking through low, close grape arbors. But as we followed the medallion's path the shadows from above shifted and the arbor slowly grew wider and taller. There were fewer leaves and the vines became thicker until we found ourselves walking on a giant vine that was as thick as a strong man's back. Our hearts rose when we felt fresh air and soon we were walking in sunshine our path rising upwards.

Trekking on the huge horizontal vine, we had to tread carefully, for the thing was round and we slipped often. But as it rose it widened and when we reached the crest we all paused to behold a wonder. Before us was a giant valley and around that valley we saw a dozen other thick vines that came from all angles and merged into a massive tree trunk far below is in the center of a placid crystal blue lake. From where the trunk sprang, another trunk also grew out, just as big as the other one and yet it was the brown color of the tap-root that grew in the tangled maze.

We descended down to the lake and then swam over to the tree. The water was pure and I couldn't resist drinking in a lot of it as I swam. As we came ashore on a giant earthy mound, I saw the little boy we had seen earlier sitting at the base of the massive Tree of Life with his arms folded and looking at us so very cross.

"You cheated!" he said. "You have a map! Cheaters!"

"No one told us the rules," Kell said as we approached him.

"Well I'm telling you now. You cheated so you lose. Go back to your stupid boat and die in the flood with everyone else."

"You know of our plight?" I asked.

"I know everything.," he said. "I know that that stupid ugly Moanmalla devil got the drop on our blessed Gavial because she was busy helping you to kill that stupid ugly Visalth creature, so it's all your fault because you needed her help and you couldn't even kill a stupid bone-dragon by yourself because you're stupid.

"And you witch," he went on. "It's all your fault because you got yourself kidnapped and you needed a stupid Paladin to help you because you're too dumb to help yourself and all this is because of you and you started it. He then turned to me. And you Longo el-stupido."

"I know," I said holding up my hands. "It's my fault because I'm ugly and stupid."

"And you smell."

"I know," I nodded. "I smell worse than a mangy dog rolling in dead fish."

The boy started to giggle.

"You smell worse than a dead dog that's been rotten three days and then rolled up in dead fish."

"I smell worse than a bloated dead pig left in the sun till it explodes!" I exclaimed gleefully.

"You smell worse," the boy laughed, "worse than a whole pile of dead bloated pigs left in the sun a hundred days and then exploding -- Bsssshhhh!"

"I smell worse," I said raising an eyebrow and leaning in toward him, "than a camel fart."

"Ohhhpp!"

He covered his mouth and his eyes went wide as he giggled and danced in circles.

"A camel fart," I added, "after he's eaten a pile of monkey poop."

The boy broke into peals of childish laughter. His delight was contagious as he kept laughing and pointing, causing even Kell and Wendfala to chuckle.

"What you said!" he cried. "What you said!"

"What? Camel farts or monkey poop?"

The boy fell down rolling in glee. Kell and Wendfala eyed me.

"I have two small cousins," I said. "This could go on for hours."

"You're funny," the child said finally as he rose. "I'm gonna call you Longo el-funnio."

"Why not el-farto?" I asked? ripping out a good one.

The little boy laughed uproariously. Kell and Wendfala just smiled, shaking their heads.

"Okay," the boy said wiping the tears from his eyes. "Okay you pass the test."

"Test?" I asked curiously.

"You stand in the Sacred Tree of Life itself. You want a blessing from the Angel. The least you can do is to show us that you have some life in you. Too many people take life too seriously. Life is to be savored and enjoyed. True life can't happen without laughing sometimes, no matter how dire the time. So I'll help you go to see the Angel of Life. But to do that I have to pause the world."

"I – I don't understand?" I said.

"That's just because you're stupid," the boy said slipping back into being a brat. "I am the Angel's protector. I could let you in to see Gavreel, but that would drain the life from you. I mean you are mortals, no offense."

"None taken."

"So I have to pause the world just a moment so that your life would stand still and couldn't be drained. To do that I need some sands of time."

"And where would I find these sands of time?" I asked.

"On the Island of Chronis of course."

Kell was about to speak but the boy held up his hand.

"Your Master," he said, "is about to moan and groan about how far away it is and blah, blah, blah. But there is a way, and so I leave it to you, Longo el-farto. You happily landed on the only point on this island that would allow you to get into the maze. My beach."

"Yes," I said . "And?"

"I hear that you're cunning. Figure it out."

"Why?" I cried. "Why can't you just tell us? Why must it be a yet another riddle?"

"Because that's the rules, el-farto."

"What rules? Whose rules?"

"It's in all the stories and legends and myths. The hero always has to work out all kinds of riddles and puzzles to prove that he's smart and cunning and, you know, just smart and cunning and like that."

"Who says?"

"I just told you!" he said stomping his foot. "The legends. The stories and all of that."

"Yeah," I said eying him. "Well what if the legends and the stories lied?" Huh? He exclaimed.

"What if the people in those myths and legends just made all that stuff up just to make themselves look smart and cunning? Huh? You ever think about that?"

"No, because it's in the stories, so it has to be true."

"Were you there?" I asked seriously.

"No."

"So how do you know, smarty?" I asked. "What if they had help sometimes and just didn't tell? What if they just made stuff up to make themselves look good. Ever think of that?"

He just looked at me, his lips twitching, his head bobbing to the side. I pressed.

"So," I said. "So how come you can't help us?"

"'Cause it'd be cheating."

"Cheating only counts in games," I said. "Cheating doesn't count if your life is on the line. You ever had your life on the line?"

"Sure," he said. "Lots of times."

"Name one."

"I can't remember," he said. "There's been too many."

"You ever cheat?" I asked, looking him dead in the eye.

He looked a little troubled. Then he placed his hands on his hips and said, "So what if I did?"

"So what if you cheated now?"

We stood there. I knew how to cock my head just right to stare him down, the same look Kell had used on many plenty of times before. I had him, but he wouldn't budge. So I tried the ultimate weapon.

"What's the matter?" I asked. "You afraid?" I then flapped my arms about like a chicken.

He looked down for just an instant and then looked back up. There was resolve in his eyes, and his nostrils flared just a little, and then he stood a little taller.

"No," he said.

Then he spit on his hand and held it out. I spit on mine and we clasped and shook. And even as I made friends with some sort of young looking deity, the world around me began to glitter and sparkle. I felt a sudden sensation of swift motion while the shimmering engulfed me. And then I was on a beach. It was a different beach. It had a different shape than the one on which we had landed on, but the vines and the water were the same.

Kell and Wendfala stood beside me astonished as I. The boy was by the shore. He held his fingers to his teeth and whistled. Then from way down at the far side of the beach there came the pounding of hooves. In a moment we saw two winged horses galloping on the sand. One was a steed and as black as night. The other was a mare and had the color of ripe chestnuts in autumn.

"Pegasus?" Kell breathed.

"Pegasus's," Wendfala said in wonder.

They looked eager to see the boy and when they stopped before him they whinnied and bowed and nuzzled. The boy spoke softly to the horses. They snorted some then they looked at us. The mare's flank rippled and her wings gave a quick flutter. The boy spoke some more. The steed stamped.

"They think that you stink too," the boy said. "But they're okay. They know the way to the island, but when you get there they will stay on the beach waiting for your return."

"They're beautiful," I said.

"They said they know," the boy said. "But they said to say thank you anyway." I smiled at them, wanting to pet one.

"So listen," the boy said. "You gotta promise to get them back before sunset tomorrow. I mean it."

"Okay," I said. "Promise."

"Okay then. I better get to my nap time."

"Okay. And thanks."

"Wait," Wendfala said. "The sands of time – how much? How much do you need?"

"As much as you can carry," the boy shrugged.

And with that he sparkled away.

Chapter 5: Chronis

The mare strode up to us, her eyes straight on my master.

"I know you," she said in a voice that spoke in all our minds. "You are of Kyrinna; a holy woman who helped in the time of the Welting Waste. She was a good woman, strong and true."

"That was long before my time," my master said. "I know her only from family lore"

"Yet she shadows your soul," the mare said.

"And so honors my quest."

The steed snorted.

"Your quest rests on the edge of a knife blade," he said. Moanmalla promised ninety-nine days, but soon enough her curse will wash away whole islands. Already stores of food in houses and root-cellars around the Nine are beginning to rot. If you were to stop this devastation tomorrow your lands would still face ruin."

"So why do we talk?" Kell asked. "Tomorrow is getting closer."

"Spoken like Kyrinna," the mare whinnied. "Climb on."

Kell mounted the mare while Wendfala and I took to the steed, sitting just before his broad wings. The two horses turned and began to gallop to the shore line. Their hooves splashed sand and then water even as the steeds began to work their wings. I could feel the power of the beast run through me. As he raced faster and faster I saw the splashes get smaller and smaller until it was as if he were galloping over the water itself. Then with a great lunge I felt something in my stomach heave and the Pegasus tucked his legs.

Behind me the powerful wings clove through the air and the tickling inside of me was a delight as we climbed higher and higher. Wendfala, at my back, held me close and let loose a squeal of glee. The water below us sparkled in the sunshine and the feeling was unlike anything that I had ever known. The whole world came into my view as we rose and the Island of the Tree of Life became a dot in the vast ocean as we soared with the clouds.

But all around us darkness loomed. Moanmalla's curse could not touch the blessed place of the Tree of Life, but the rest of the Realms were not so sacred. As we neared the wall of the storm ahead, I saw the clouds where lit by the sun and were glowing brilliantly, with silver rains coming down in raging torrents.

Far behind us to the north, the dark was marked by explosions of lightning as the storm intensified.

Our Pegasus soared even higher and it was as if my breath was being taken away. His magic must have been truly strong, for even as we raced I felt hardly any wind rush past me. We climbed above the storm and the scene before me was so beautiful. The clouds were enormous bright puffs that cast shadows on each other, so that some places liked like beautiful bursts of snow while dark shadowy canyons ranged between them. Lightning leapt from cloud to cloud and I could hear the low roll of thunder almost constantly.

We flew on with a speed that was clearly magical. The storm below quickly faded to nothing but little white streams in advance of the moving front. To my left I saw a mass of land that just beginning to feel the effects of the massive storm. I thought of someone far below cursing the luck as their picnic plans were being spoiled and I thought my master wise in not raising an alarm. One can prepare for an army, but what could one do about a flood?

A smattering of islands came into view, looking so lovely in the ocean. They quickly sped away and then there was nothing but open sea and clear blue sky. The moon had risen in the dusky sky before us and its light dappled the waters. The Pegasus' magic had taken us well away from any places known to our charts or maps, and I wondered how far we had come and where we were. The air around us began to turn cool as we rushed into twilight. I scanned the sea below but saw nothing for miles. Then the Pegasus began to climb higher still.

Wendfala slapped my thigh and pointed ahead. There I saw yet another wonder. The Island of Chronis floated in the sky. As if some giant hand had ripped a piece of the earth and hung it there, the island in the sky was a wonder to behold. It was a lush and verdant land with rolling hills and valleys. There seemed to be paths or streams wandering those vales and I thought I saw a scattering of houses. Deeper inland the hills rose to small jagged mountains. The sky above was a deep, beautiful blue and the moon behind the mountains looked as if it had grown ten times.

From one mountain I saw a river thread its way down, growing and winding along the valleys until it had flowed to the very edge of the island and tumbled off in a stunning waterfall that dispersed into vapor in which arched a vivid rainbow. Below I saw the bones of the land all rocky and craggy, torn jagged and ripped. As we neared I saw something dark and wispy streaming from the pointed rocky center.

The island loomed larger and larger and then I saw a crystal shoreline just ahead of us. The Pegasus lowered his mighty legs and began galloping, and I thought that I saw the very air itself splashing under his hoofs. I heard the soft pounding of surf but saw no water as we galloped onto the glittering sands.

We all dismounted, somewhat reluctantly, as that had been quite an incredible ride. For a while we did not speak and just took in the moment and admired the awesome beauty all around us. From that far shore we looked across an ocean of sky. Wisps of feathery clouds floated all about. The sky above was the dark of night and sheets of stars twinkled, and yet we were lit as if in a lovely June evening. Before us the sun shone like a small yellow ball on a mist of rusty red, its rays stretching far on either side, but its light barely warming us.. Behind us the moon loomed beyond the mountains and bathed us in its cool glow. All around us the air itself was crisp and clean and tinged with blue.

"That path," the mare said in our minds, pointing with her wing, "will take you where you need to be. No harm will come to you in this land if you act wisely. Go now and do not tarry. We must leave when we must leave and if you are not with us you will be marooned. Now go."

Thanking them we turned and started jogging along the sandy path into the grass beyond. The ground on this island was something of a strange delight, for every time my feet touched the ground it was as though it shifted below and then bounced up to give me an extra boost in my step. Indeed, the land itself seemed to be slowly and gently rocking and bobbing. We came upon what I thought to be a small stream, but it was anything but. It was like the land had cracked and air was flowing between the banks. The rushing air almost had substance, but we could see through it down past the island roots and to the distant ocean below.

We came to a place where our path was crossed by such a chasm and we hesitated. It was an easy leap, but the sheer breath of the fall below was enough to make one wonder. Kell was the first to make the jump and as he did our side of the ground shifted away some as if he had kicked off of a raft. We watched amazed and the land slowed and then drifted back into place. Then Wendfala and I clasped hands and made our leap, then watched again as the island shifted.

Deeper inland the walking was firmer. As we followed the path shrubs and trees began to grow. We rounded one hill and we saw a small cottage. Smoke rose from its chimney and we called out, but no one came. We saw more little houses as we walked and while there were signs of life no one was at home.

Then we came to a place where the path became a road. A walled city stood in the distance. We ran. The city seemed alive, for we saw more rising smoke and smelled exotic aromas. As we reached the gates we found them open and welcoming, but there were no guards or watchers. Again we called and again there was no answer.

Inside the city we were completely baffled. Carts full of fresh produce or sacks of wheat or crated goods were all about on the main street but no one tended them. There was a small café with tables outside. The tables were set with food and drink but there was no one sitting. We saw one mug of tea still steaming.

"What is this place?," I pondered aloud. "It's as though all of the people vanished the moment we appeared. I can't believe that everyone here is so shy."

"I sense no magic," Wendfala said. "Neither fair nor foul."

"It's a mystery indeed," Kell said. "But it's a mystery we will have to ponder on later. Time passes and we have a quest. Let's make haste."

Again we ran and again I felt my master's Ancestor strength as we raced almost as fast as the Pegasus' flew. Beyond the empty city there were empty farms, fields, and groves. Beyond them the mountain loomed and signs of life seemed to be just disappearing before they could see them.

In and among the foothills were more streams and then rivers of air. We crossed those over wobbly bridges of ropes and wooden slats. Our path led along one wide river that was flowing so thick that we could almost see the air underneath it, and it had bits of twigs and leaves rolling along in the strong current. The river path led along a valley between two small mountains. As the way curved to our right, the river grew broader and slower until we found ourselves at the edge of a vast mountain lake. A small breeze blew here and it was as if I could see wisps of the lake air being sprayed like white-caps on the sea.

Far in the distance, in the middle of the lake, was an island. It looked as if it were a plateau whose top we could not see. From the center of that island we saw rays of light reaching in a broad column to the heavens. The light was all streaked with grey lines.

The path wound around the edge of the air lake. There was no shore, no gentle sloping, just sheer cliffs that reached down for a mile. Below, the clouds floated by and below them we saw the distant glint of the ocean bathed in the blue of the moon. The lake's island bottom was like a rough cone reaching well beyond the cliffs. From its center we saw a fine dusty mist falling and scattering on the winds below.

"The sands of time," my master said as we gazed at the sight. "They stream down from the heavens to this place at the center of all things. Here they gather and are dispersed by the winds of our world."

"So then," Wendfala said, "that island is our goal. But I don't think that I'd want to try my luck swimming in air."

"There's a bridge," I said pointing.

A ways ahead and up a tall tor we saw thin lines stretching across the lake to a tower on the island. As the bridge stretched, it sagged low so that it almost touched the lake. We scampered up the craggy rocks and to the top of the pinnacle. There was a flat landing and a rope bridge. The bridge and the crossing looked terrifying.

Two cables as wide as a man's hand span were slung from tor to tower. Beneath them was a single rope as thick as my arm forming a triangle with the other two ropes. Between the larger ropes was woven hemp. To me it looked as though the hemp was simply for stability, for it would be of no use as a net were one to slip off the tightrope crossing.

"How the hell are we –"

"One foot after the other," Kell said, grabbing the hand holds. "And don't look down."

But how could one not look? One foot after the other was fine enough, but I had to see where I stepped, and when I looked down my brain reeled. As we trod carefully, the bridge sagged and we were sloping downwards. It was a strange thing to see my feet walking over rippling air and fine clouds beneath me. I had to look but I desperately tried not to lose my balance.

My master was in the lead and Wendfala was before me. I kept my eyes on my clunky boots and her delicate silk slippers. We were nearing a low point in the bridge's sag and I watched the hem of her skirt fluttering. Far below the ocean sparkled.

Then my heart froze as I saw her foot slip. She cried out and her leg was hanging. My instinct was to reach out for her, but as terror gripped my heart my hands gripped the cables. She lost her other foot and she screamed as she flailed. The bridge started rocking.

"Stop!" Kell shouted. "Easy. Easy woman. Your own panic will kill you."

She calmed. She hung by her hand, her legs dangling. The bridge too calmed. It's swaying ceased and all was still. Wendfala strained to lift herself and soon she had one foot, then the other back on the rope. She righted herself and we all took a deep breath.

"This will not do," Kell said. "We crawl like frightened children when our need is for courage and speed."

"What are you saying?" I asked.

"I am saying that we trust my Ancestor's Strength. We run.

“What?”

But my master was off like lightening. With long swift strides he raced up along the far end of the bridge. Wendfala turned to me, raised an eyebrow and shrugged. She sped away and by the time she was halfway up the other side Kell had reached the tower.

I took a deep breath and put my fate in the Ancestor’s strength. I ran. I ran without thinking, my legs taking long swift strides while my hands gripped the stays and helped propel me. My toes would barely touch down before I leapt forward like a deer through the woods. As I gained on the far end it became more like climbing but the strength kept me speeding me along.

“Well done,” Kell smiled, slapping me on the back. “We should call you Longo the sure-foot.”

“You should keep a list of all the names people give me.” I said with a smirk.

“You should see this,” Wendfala said in a low and reverent tone.

We turned. The island was a crater. The light streaming up from its smooth sides rose to the purple sky and then splayed out to the far reaches of space. So thick was that light that it looked almost solid. In the center of the light there was an hourglass with no glass.

The sands of time floated down through that light and gathered on a whirling bulb held by nothing. The ball of dust flowed down to a trickling point, where grain by grain the sands dropped to the lower bulb where the stuff swirled in the opposite direction. From there it funneled and dripped to the winds below.

There was a winding stair carved into the crater walls. We hurried down. As we raced, I thought I saw something floating in the bottom bulb. The stairs brought us lower and once we got closer the thing in the sands became a person, a woman. She looked to be swimming in the swirling eddy, straining to keep away from the bottom. The stairs took us to a place along the middle of the huge lower bulb where there was what seemed to be a giant altar set on a dais.

“What is she doing there?” I wondered aloud.

“Might that woman have been the sacrifice?” Wendfala asked.

“That is yet another mystery that we don’t have time to solve,” Kell said.

But even as we spoke the woman in the sand saw us as she whirled by. Her face lit up and she began screaming, frantic silent screams trying to swim against the flow to us.

“I have seen that face,” Kell said. “Could it be – it couldn’t be.”

“Anna!” I cried.

Chapter 6: All We Could Carry

I wept with tears of joy and sorrow. Truly it was Anna, but she was a grown woman. I saw her face as she battled the swirling sands and she was pleading, calling my name. I reached for her but Kell stayed my arm. Anna soon lost her battle and was swept away to whirl again in the sands.

"We must save her," I cried. "She's aging. She'll die an old woman in there and then turn to dust. Master we must do something to save her."

Kell took up Ashrune. Anna was on the far side. As she spun again toward us Kell plunged the large hammer into the eddy. There was a sudden roar of wind and Anna grasped at the head. She caught it and we could hear her screaming in pain. She suddenly let go, and as she spun away I saw her clutching her hands and moaning. Kell pulled Ashrune out and the hammer head was smoking, covered in rust and pitted. The crater was silent again.

"Curse me for an idiot," he said. "I should have realized that magic does not age well,"

"What do we do?" Wendfala wailed. "She will surely die."

"I don't know!" Kell cried through grit teeth.

But I knew and I didn't care what it cost me. As Anna wheeled around again I shoved my arm deep into the sands of time. I screamed. It was like plunging into scalding hot water, but the instant I felt Anna's hands clutch my own I knew that I had to endure the agony. The roar of the rushing wind returned as I held onto my friend for dear life. It took all the strength of my body and spirit to hold her in the torrent. I felt myself being pulled in and I screamed with the pain.

My master and Wendfala clutched me and the three of us pulled with all our might. Slowly we gained ground as the vortex began to give up its captive. My arm was almost all out and the air around was a cooling relief. In a moment Anna's hand appeared and my heart leapt with joy. Then we had her arm and Kell grabbed it quickly. Hand over hand he pulled and then her other arm was free and clutching us.

Slowly but surely we drew her out, and when I saw her lovely face I was sure that we had saved her. The more of her naked body that the vortex gave up the easier she slid out. The sands finally relented and gave us back our Anna. Grains of sand slid from her body and streamed from her long auburn hair and got sucked back into their home in the vortex.

The moment that Anna set her first foot on the ground, Wendfala let go of me and I felt her rummaging through my rucksack. I paid her no heed as my precious Anna stepped out and hugged me and Kell, breathing heavily and weeping in joy. Then the three of us embraced in a giant hug and she felt so real and good and warm.

"Don't move," Wendfala said.

Then I heard tiny tinkling sounds. Kell began to laugh. I looked and I saw that the witch had taken the old goblet from my pack. It was a trophy that I had gathered back in Galth, the lair of Visalth the Bone-Dragon. She was using it to gather up some sand that was streaming from Anna's hair. When the cup was full, she capped it with her hand and Anna stepped away. The sands were still flying from her as we wept and embraced. But in that embrace my arm was in some serious pain.

"Thank you," Anna wept over and over. "You saved me. You saved me."

We gave her water and she drank as one parched for days. I gazed on her. She was no longer the skinny wiry imp I had known. She was a grown woman and looked all of it. But her wide green eyes and her pointed nose were still the same and her smile could still warm me all over. Kell gave her his cloak and she wrapped herself in it, blushing. She then drank some more water, taking long and deep swallows.

Kell rolled up my sleeve and looked to my arm. I was withered from my bicep to my fingers, my hand was like the claw of an old man. I could barely lift it and it pained me to try. It was agony making a fist.

"There is no healing for age," Kell said as he fashioned a sling. "I'm sorry lad."

"This arm has been a curse," I muttered, "might as well add Longo the withered to your list."

"Oh my dear Longo," Anna said, kissing my shrunken hand. "To save me you have lost your arm. How can I ever repay you?"

"It's just an arm," I said. "I have another."

"But how could this happen?" she said. "How is it that you found me here? Where's my sister? And – and who is this?"

"This is our friend Wendfala," Kell said. "But stories must wait. The day grows short and we need to get back to the crystal shore before the Pegasus' leave us."

"But—"

"Now," he said

We turned to the stairs but we had not taken three steps when Wendfala cried out.

"Kell wait," she said. "The sands in the cup are burning my hand. It's like they want to return to their winds. It burns."

Kell took the leather pouch from his belt and tossed the coins away. He held it open over the cup. The instant Wendfala took her hand away the sands began streaming back to the vortex. Quickly he capped the goblet and tied it off tight. The sands bumped and beat on their trap. He wrapped the thing tight in a bandage and stuffed it deep in my pack. Anna bathed Wendfala's palm with some water and we were off again in haste.

It was clear that despite the Ancestor's strength, Anna was still weak and disoriented so Kell carried her. Crossing the rope bridge with his precious cargo, my master was nimble as a gazelle and steady as a mountain goat. My own crossing was one-armed but this time I didn't look down. I trusted my feet and felt more than saw my way as I ran like a madman. I could feel the goblet in my rucksack bouncing wildly.

On our race back to the crystal shore we never stopped to wonder or question. We followed the path through fields and farms, over gaping rivers of air, through the town with no one there, along the quiet streams and through the grass land all the way without stopping, running the whole way. But when our feet finally crunched beneath the glittering sands on the shore, the Pegasus's were gone.

I stood amazed. My brain went blank. My mind refused to believe it. Wendfala crumbled to her knees. Kell let Anna slide to the sand and strode to the darkening shore. He peered a moment, and then crying out in a rage that would of scared the hounds of hell. He then whirled the battered Ashrune over his head so fast that it shrieked through the air. And then he flung it away. It sailed far over the ocean of air and was lost to sight.

I wanted to weep. I wanted to weep for the four hopeless stranded mortals, but more I wanted to weep for my master and his final foolish act of despair. Yet I found that in this point in my wretched life I had no more tears. My eyes itched bit, but I didn't even bother to scratch. I hung my head low and Wendfala did my weeping for me. Anna looked around at the magnificent astral beauty around her, not knowing her doom.

Then I heard a small sound in the distance like a soft whistling. I looked up and there was a speck in the sky. Kell raised his arm and Ashrune landed back in his grip. A moment later I saw soft white and black dots growing closer. Called by my master's hammer the Pegasus' had returned.

"We're saved!" I cried.

"Move!" Kell shouted when the Pegasus had finally gotten close.

The mare wheeled toward me, her hooves barely touching the ground. I grabbed Wendfala with my good hand and leapt a mighty leap. A moment later we were back in the sky, the witch clutching me for dear life, now crying tears of joy. Off to my left Kell held Anna on the steed. The look of awe on the girl's face was priceless.

I saw little of our journey back to the Island of the Sacred Tree. I was surrounded by the beauty of the Earth's ocean at dusk. The sun was a glowing ball in the west and before us a myriad of stars sparkled in the the sky. But I was near exhaustion and it was all I could do to stay awake.

In time I felt the mare begin to descend. That lovely delight tickled my loins as we flew lower and slower. I saw the island in the twilight loom closer and closer, and then I felt the mare's hooves thud, splashing the shore.

"We made it," I breathed.

"We did," she said.

I slumped to the sand and saw the sun slide into the sea as sleep overtook me.

In the morning I was the last to wake. Wendfala gave me water, biscuits and cheese. I was happy for the simple fare. Kell was telling Anna our tale. She was still wrapped in only his cloak, but she looked as beautiful as ever, more so as a woman. I joined them and she fluttered her eyes shyly at me, clutching her cloak tighter.

"And now," Kell said. "What of you? Tell us your story?"

"I can't say much," she said. "Gavial was nice. She told us stories and she sang us songs. She was nice. For a while. Then one day she got this weird look on her face. Then she just stopped talking. She just sat there like a lump. She wouldn't talk, she wouldn't do anything. In time Anna even poked her and she didn't even do anything."

It was strange seeing Anna as a woman and yet hearing a child.

"We thought she was sick or something. We didn't know what to do. Then she suddenly jumped up and shouted 'No'! Anna and I didn't know what to do. Then this huge sword just appeared in her hand and she jumped up and out of the shrine. Then there was all kinds of thunder and lightning above us. Anna and I, we raced upstairs and we saw Gavial fighting with a – with like a storm.”

“A storm?” Kell said.

“Yeah but – but it had a shape, like a monster. It had tornados for legs and they were tearing up all the gravestones and it had arms made of clouds and lightning and it had lightning coming out of its fingers and Gavial was fighting the lightning with her sword and it was so scary.”

“Go on.”

“So then, so then the big statues started to crumble and Gavial was screaming like she was in pain. I think she got hit by the lightning because she was staggering back. Then a big chunk of statue fell and I jumped out of the way and I didn’t see what happened to Anna. And then the whole place shook as the Angel fell to her knees and started yelling in some strange language. Then the world around me seemed to whirl, and it was like I got sucked out of the grotto, and then it got really weird.”

I was hanging on her every word, trying to imagine the horror.

“It was like something was pulling me,” she went on. “Pulling me up and up and up until I was floating. And I really was floating in space because I could look down and see the whole world below me. It was kind of cool in a way. But then it got real creepy and I got pulled down and down by this big light and then it got even weirder.

“It was like,” she said scrunching her face. “It was like I was nothing. I was floating in the light and it was as if I was the sand. I whirled around a while and then I sort of fell, drop by drop, and when all the drops had gathered in the whirlwind I became – I became a baby.”

She told of how she watched herself slowly grow in the sands from an infant to a child. When she reached her real age she started to remember everything and then she began to grow older. She realized what was happening. She had tried to break free, but soon learned it was futile. I had finally resigned myself to the fact that I was going to grow old and die in there.

“I’d become dust,” she said with a faraway look in her eyes. “And then I’d fall to the world and that would be the end of me.”

She was silent a moment. Then she shuddered and shook herself.

“But that didn’t happen,” she said smiling. “You saved me. And now it’s kind of cool being all grown up. Kind of cool indeed.

"Gavial rescued you," Kell said. "By flinging you into the charm of the astral sphere, she hid you in a place where the demon could never find you."

"But, but what of my sister?" Anna asked. "You tell me that the demon has her and Gavial. Do you think there's any chance for her?"

"Who are you?" a mysterious voice challenged suddenly.

I looked about and we were once again standing on the trunk of the Tree of Life. The little angel boy guardian was there with his arms folded looking at Anna.

"Who are you?" she replied.

"I asked first." he said.

"I am Anna."

"No you're not," the boy said. "You're the Other Anna. How stupid can you be if you don't know your own name?"

"I am older now," Anna said. "So I get to be Anna."

"That's so dumb."

"And you are a brat."

"And you're so stupid. You're all wrapped up in a heavy cloak. Don't you even know the sun's out?"

Anna cocked her head and opened the cloak. The boy's eyes near popped from his head for a moment and he turned beet red and shut his eyes.

"Ewww!" he squealed.

"Enough," Kell said. Anna closed her wrap. "We have followed your wishes and we have brought back our treasure."

"Okay," the boy said opening his eyes. "Give it to me."

I slung my pack and Wendfala reached in and drew out the wrapped goblet. But even as she held it for the boy we all looked and we gaped.

"Kell?" she said.

There was a small burn in the bandage. She held the goblet by the stem while he quickly unwrapped it. Beneath we saw that the leather had been stretched and it too had a small hole. The boy started to laugh. Carefully my master undid the leather and looked inside. There was not a speck. Desperate, we searched my pack, but there too we saw the tiny burn hole. Bit by bit the sands had escaped.

"You can't even hold onto some sand," the boy mocked as he danced and laughed. "You guys are the stupidest mortals I've ever seen."

I stood speechless. Anna fell into Wendfala's arms.

"What does this mean?" she asked.

"It means your whole stupid world's gonna drown," the boy jeered.

Kell grabbed me by the shoulders.

"Longo, look at me!"

I did, I was frightened and I began to sputter and apologize. I believed that he thought it was all my fault and I felt crushed in his probing stare, but he hushed me. He kept peering at me, ignoring the taunting child.

"Longo," he said, "forgive me for what I must do."

"What must you do master?"

"Cast your mind back," he said, "and make you remember. Remember the woman in the water."

"Master no!"

"Selivanova," he said softly. "See her, Longo."

"Master please!"

"Kell!" Wendfala cried. "Why do you torment the boy?"

"See her Longo. See that fair and sorrowful face. Remember how she begged you. Remember how she pleaded. Remember how she wailed in her horrible doom."

I tried to tear away but his grip was like iron. I shut my eyes and turned my head as the angst welled in my soul. I did see her. I saw her as if she were real and I felt her misery. I remembered the longing to help the pitiful girl and the feeling of hopeless regret welled in my soul even as the tears welled in my eyes.

As if from far away I heard my master call for the witch, and then Wendfala gasped. Then something touched my cheek, dabbed and then my master embraced me as a father would comfort a child. I felt his warmth and I felt his love. I looked up at him with blurry eyes.

"Master why?"

Kell smiled sadly and looked to the boy. He stood stunned. Wendfala held the corner of the handkerchief to him.

"I see seven, no eight grains," Wendfala said. "Motes of the sands of time trapped by his tears and captured by sorrow. It was all that we could carry."

Chapter 7: Damned

The boy was true to his word, begrudging as he was about it. He carefully picked the tiny grains from Wendfala's handkerchief and dropped them in his palm. He breathed a gentle breath on them and a small ball began to glow. It was a slow warm glow and the boy kept blowing gently as if fanning kindling, and as he did the light brightened. At first it was a soft white light, but as it grew in size it began to swirl with pale hues. The colors rose up a little, but the boy kept his hand where it was. The light hung in the air a moment and the colors became crisper. Thin tendrils appeared. Eight of them seemed to be probing the air like insect feelers. They reached toward us and I took a step back. The filaments stretched and reached for us, and as they did they grew thicker. The air shuddered before me and as I tried to take another step away I couldn't move.

The air became thick and it was hard to breathe. The colorful strings were all about me and I was awash in their changing light. Suddenly I couldn't breathe but – but I didn't need to breathe. I couldn't move but I didn't need to move. I thought that I should be afraid but I could not find any fear inside of me. I felt as if I were nestled and snug, almost as if I were adrift in warmth and comfort. My eyes were fixed forward and all I could see was the whirlwind of those threads of ever changing colors.

Then something beyond the colors stirred, as if the air beyond my cocoon of light had been shaken. It seemed to tremble all about me, but I knew that I was safe. Then the swirling colors began to spin faster and faster. I thought that I should have felt the speed of the wind that they would have made, but there was none. It was silent. As fast as they came, the threads and their colors washed away and I was gazing into the purest white I had ever seen. The white seemed to be infinite in its depth, and looking into it gave me the sense that I was falling.

"Fear not," a voice said from everywhere and nowhere.

It was an indescribable sound. It was light and somehow harsh, melodic and yet discordant, soothing and at the same time terrible, and in those two simple words my soul seemed filled with a well of conflicting emotions and I was at once joyful and in despair, calm and anxious, soothed and excited.

"What is life but a trial of contradictions?" the voice from everywhere said. "There can be no hope without fear. To be happy one must know sorrow. To know love is to know hate and to live is to die."

I gaped into the brilliant void as the words flew around me. A form began to appear in the distance. It was the form of a cherub angel gleefully flying and playing, but even as I stared, the cherub turned into a winged skeleton and then turned into an angel bathed in blue that was pouring silver water from a golden vase. Then that angel became draped in darkness and clutched a long scythe.

"You seek a Blessing from Gavreel, the Angel of Life, but I say to you that the Angel has already blessed you with life. What more can I bestow? You would beg advantage over the demon who I will not name, but what would that boon be? Wisdom? Fortitude? Power? Courage? Strength? You would need all of these and more, for truly the Steed spoke true and the one who will not be named cannot now be stopped."

Wrapped as I was in the comfort of the Angel, my heart quailed. The shifting form in the void was now the cherub and the little child looked at me with a tear in its eye.

"There is wisdom in that thought," the voice said. "And there is also wisdom in knowing that your foe is so much like you. You have the Strength of the Paladin Ancestors, but you would have that tenfold were you to head into the storm. Your power and fortitude lies in your unity, as does your courage.

"Your challenge is great and your goal is good. So take this small token of Gavreel's love and trust, and face your foe knowing that my blessing is in my words, and remember that the shadow of my sister still lies in you. *Vade in pace, revertar in pace, et pacis erit vobiscum.*"

With those words the bright white void began to crack. Fissures appeared, splitting the image with many shifting colors, and then it was as though I was hurled a thousand miles away.

When my breath came back it was dark. Bright stars shone above but the land on which I stood was not the Island of the Tree of Life. It was a harsh place full of scraggly dead trees with the smell of decay. I breathed deeply and felt a surging inside of me, as if there was something pent up, charged and waiting to be let loose. There was an energy in me, and it was as if I shared that energy with the others.

Kell stood confident and knowing. His mighty Warhammer Ashrune had been healed and my master's face was set with a grave look. Somehow I knew, as certain as I knew my name, that the Angel had granted him wisdom.

Wendfala seemed to glow from within and her eyes sparkled. She looked as if she could beat down the gates of hell, even if it took her a hundred years to do so.

What I saw in Anna should have shocked me, but in that same instant I understood. She was clothed in a flowing blue gown like the Angel in my vision. She was at once beautiful, regal, and proud, and yet her face was forlorn and she looked like one doomed.

The others turned to me and for a moment I felt almost as if the Angel had neglected me. But then Anna pointed to my hand. I wore a fingerless leather gauntlet trimmed and decked with silver that wrapped up to my forearm. I moved my withered arm with ease and flexed my fingers. I felt powerful energy flowing in my hand and I instinctively pointed my arm upwards, a bolt of lightning blasting forth from my fingertips. I gaped in amazement.

"The Angel thinks highly of you lad," Kell smiled. "Our virtues are in our character, while yours lies in your arm."

"I suspect then," Wendfala said with a smirk, "that his inner qualities need no help."

"Longo can be simplicity itself," Anna said. "Yet he has a soul that is, if not pure... righteous."

"My soul would rest easier," I said, "if I knew where we were and why. What is this place?"

"This is Mortui-horas." Kell said. "The Land of the Dead Hours."

"What hours?"

"The hours of our life Gavreel wants us to be in. Look."

He pointed to the sky and it was like I was looking down. It was as if we were birds in flight, who saw sunshine gleaming on a harsh desert landscape. The winds swept over shifting dunes that had no shadow. I saw two figures huddling in the sand and then a little ways away a bone-dragon flew by.

"Visalth?" I gasped. "The dragon lives?"

"In these hours he does," Kell chuckled. "Look, see the two people shaking the dust from their clothes? That is you and I."

"Indeed, we are seeing our own dead hours. But pay attention."

The scene flew by over a vast ocean and for a while we saw nothing but water. And then a small island came into view. We soared down and through an open cave and it was Gavial's sacred grotto. As we wheeled past we saw the Angel of Glory singing to two children. Anna shut her eyes and turned away.

But then we flew beyond the shrine and soon we were deep in jagged mountains. One mountain was like a volcano but belched no fire. From its cone there erupted dark clouds that gathered in the sky whirling and forming, taking the shape of a monster with storms for legs and arms alive with lightening.

"Anna!" I cried.

The girl looked and gasped.

"That's her," she said. "That's the thing that attacked Gavial!"

"The Angel of Life spoke true," Kell said. "When finally we met her we were too late to stop the demon's destruction. But here and now we might prevent her curse from ever beginning."

"But how?" I asked. "We are where we were in the beginning, but the puzzle still remains; how do we battle a storm? How do you stop the rain?"

"Gavreel's words," Kell mulled. "She said . . . she said *your foe is much like you.*" His brow furrowed a moment, then relaxed as a smile crept across his face. "How is a storm like a human?"

"I haven't the foggiest," I said.

"It grows!" Anna said.

"And in order to grow?"

"It must feed," Wendfala said. "And it feeds on the ocean, so we must stop it from reaching the ocean."

"It will be a war of attrition," Kell said. "We must outlast it until its energy is so drained that it must feed on itself and so die."

"And in that death all will be undone," Anna said softly.

"That is why the Angel gave you courage child," Kell said softly.

That's when I understood why she seemed so sad. There was a battle drawing neigh and Anna knew that she had no hope, no matter the outcome. The death of Moanmalla would change the course of time and the Anna that stood with us would never have been. She was doomed.

"But," Wendfala said, "how do we get there?"

"*Men are much like an Angel with only one wing,*" I said, quoting Gavial's blessing.

"Huh?" Wendfala said, then she gasped and squealed as Kell took her under his arm and they launched into the sky.

"Anna," I said offering her my left arm.

She shut her eyes, clutched me tight, and in a moment she was squealing too.

Reaching into the sky became like falling to the earth as we soared over the ocean and across the wide plains to the cursed mountains of shadow. Through tall jagged tors and over steep crags we flew as the mountain of thunder and clouds approached. The creature hovered, standing over the cone of the volcano as lightning shot up and into its gloomy form.

It might have been two hundred feet tall, maybe more. Its face was like an ape; its skull sloped with a strong dark ridge for a brow. Its arms pulsed with throbbing veins of bright blue that lit its muscled torso in constant flashes. One tornado like leg hung dangling while the other was sucking noxious vapors from the volcano. But the monster seemed asleep. Its eyes were clouded over and its arms hung limply by its side.

Kell led us closer and Anna gripped me tight. We rose up and approached the giant's dormant face. It stirred. I tensed as the cloud lids slid open and two dim balls of lightning stared at us stupidly. Kell led us around the massive face and those eyes followed us, but the beast did nothing. Kell wheeled around its head and led us to a small bluff on the side of the mountainous volcano where we landed.

"It's as I thought," he said. "The monster is still growing and Moanmalla has yet to fully possess it. We must strike now while it is still like an infant."

"But how do we strike such a creature?" I asked.

"We will be like dogs nipping at a lion's feet," he said. "We will gnaw and bite and upset and annoy. We will aggravate the thing so that it must waste energy, and once the thing is in a storming rage we must destroy the source. That will force it to flee towards the ocean, but we will hound and vex it until it spends itself.

"Anna, Wendfala, you will begin the assault. Remember that you have the Strength of the Ancestors with you. Longo, come with me."

I took my master's arm and we flew to the creature, and even as we did a rock the size of my head broke through its face. There was a small puff and the rock fell into dark cloud. The monster twitched. Another bigger rock caught the thing on the brow. It shook and opened its eyes.

"Hey you!" Anna cried in a voice that boomed and echoed. "Wake up ape-face!"

Another stone from the other direction hit him straight in the eye and the creature reared and then roared like thunder.

"You're ugly!" Wendfala cried.

"And your momma dresses you funny!" Anna laughed.

The beast raged. It looked around, and the moment it spotted Kell and me, I let loose with a bolt from my gauntlet. White lightning crackled about its face and it clutched at in anger. It wailed and flung its arms about, throwing blue lightning out randomly. Cliffs exploded and crumbled. Rocks flew in all directions as Anna and Wendfala kept leaping about.

I struck the monster in the shoulder with another powerful bolt from my gauntlet while Kell let Ashrune fly swift and true. The hammer whirled and whirled around the skull and the thing snatched and grasped, catching nothing. It kept twisting its head, trying to catch sight of the whirling hammer, and so I let go another bolt that pierced its chest, making a hole through the vapor.

Ashrune returned to my masters hand, and as soon as he caught it, he flung it away again, cleaving into the monster's skull. The beast roared, but the clouds simply reformed. He became like a child in a tantrum, flinging his lightning everywhere, and kicking his free leg at us futilely. The tornado roared and sent stones and debris pelting into us. Still we tormented the evil thing until in its rage it tore itself away from the volcano and began stomping across the mountains, desperately seeking to destroy the maddening insects tormenting it.

The moment the beast was away, Kell smiled and we flew to the edge of the mountain cone.

"Neither your bolts nor my Ashrune combined can destroy a mountain," he said. "But that thing can."

I knew my master's mind, and so I let fly streak after streak of white lightning at the creature, peppering it while Ashrune clove into its arms and legs and chest. The monster turned. Wendfala and Anna must have guessed our plan as well, for their rocks stopped coming. I sent a bolt straight into its face so that it could be sure of its aim. Then with almost a gleeful face, it flung both arms at us. We both leapt quickly away, with Kell using the power from his mighty hammer to help propel us away at great speed. Behind us, the top of the volcano was torn asunder by blue lightning and crashed into itself.

The creature's wail was almost pitiful as it realized what it had done. But even as it gazed in horror, it shuddered and seemed to collapse from within. We watched from the air in hope. Then it rose up, its maw agape and I expected a blast of thunder. But all that came forth was Moanmalla's frail voice.

"You are a fool Kell," she said. "You may vanquish me, but you will never conquer the power I serve nor will you ever understand what you face. He is not some puny mortal despot who seeks simply to conquer and kill. His cause is beyond your pathetic imaginings. He seeks what you can never fathom and he will not be stopped.

"But know this Kell, it is now you who will be the hunted. He will find you and he will find everyone who you hold dear. Then you will watch as he slowly tortures and kills everyone and everything you ever cared about. You are now the hunted, Kell . . . you are . . . damned . . ."

Then the clouds gathered and began to drift to the west. Kell and I gathered Anna and Wendfala and we gave chase, harassing and pestering the thing mercilessly. After several minutes it finally began to drift apart. One whirling leg spun off into vapor. The blue lightning dimmed and slowly started to wink out. The eyeballs rolled from their sockets and fell to the earth where they vanished. The monster faded until all that was left was a wisp of dark vapor hovering over a sandy beach. But even there it got no respite as a steady breeze scattered what was left like smoke.

Suddenly we were bathed in warm white light. The air sparkled and whirled and I felt so serene and calm that I wanted to drift off to sleep . . .

I woke to the gentle sound of waves lapping the surf and a child gently humming. I looked up. We were back of the Island of the Tree of Life. The little boy deity was playing with his sand-castle. I sat up with the others. All around us the skies were clear, bright and blue. We had done it. Moanmalla's storm had never happened.

"So," the boy said. "I guess you figure that you're pretty smart."

"I guess," Kell said.

"Well you're not."

"And why do you say that?"

"Kell," Anna said. "I shouldn't be here."

The End of Book 2

Chapter 1 : The Witch Harpy of the North

There are stories still being whispered among the people of Theugua. Stories told about creatures hiding in the darkest corners of the world. Stories told about magic that could turn good and honest men against each other, stories about deeds that are darker than even the moonless night sky. Even so, men are quick to forget. Soon those hushed stories became nothing more than children's tales told in times of peace.

For Ornsell son of Krull, that was always the case. The stories of the past were just legends that would never come to pass. He decided to start his day early and head straight into the woods to check the traps he had set the day before. As he proceeded along at a brisk pace, getting back home in time for supper was his only concern. Handling his axe with ease, he set off towards the forest. He was also planning to cut some firewood that would last him and his son, Vygarast, for a week on his way back home.

Day excursions into the forest west of Midvein were ordinary for the village people. Though the winters up north of Theugua tended to be harsh and unforgiving, the men and women of Midvein were tough. They knew that the best way to survive the cold winds of the north was to be prepared for anything.

The morning dew had covered everything in the forest with a sparkling veil under the rising sun. Ornsell had his hands folded in front of him on his chest to try and keep himself warm. Taking a deep breath every five strides or so, he soon found himself deep in the woods and his exertions made the chill less now.

Winter mornings are the best remedy for an old man's head like mine. This is as good day as any to explore deeper into the forest, how many good days yet until I can't take a walk into the forest without needing Vygarast to help me? He laughed on the outside at the thought of being helped through the forest.

His eldest and only son was destined to be a Bard, one trained by a living legend, Lanarast the Bold. Being around to take care of him was not in his son's plans. *So be it!* He laughed it off. *If Vygarast's fate is to sing in the kings' courts and charm women with his voice for the rest of his life, then so be it.* However, a sudden frown and flush of emotion betrayed that thought. Memories of his life as a Bard (an amateur one that it was) kept interfering with his expectations for his talented young son.

You can't be jealous of your own son Ornsell. He has talent where you only had luck to rely on. Just get over it! With a quick shake of his head, he kept on heading deeper into the forest, sometimes choosing to follow the forest path, other times getting away from it. The forest was beautiful and full of life despite the chill. However, Ornsell could not get his son out of his mind. Lost in his own thoughts he ventured deeper into the woods. It was only after hearing a twig snap behind him that he jerked suddenly aware, his thoughts alarmed. He turned around only to see the dark shadows cast by the trees dance around him on the ground. Even if he couldn't see it, something felt wrong to him.

Bears are still asleep this late in the winter and it's too early into the day for the wolves to hunt. Normally, Ornsell was not a man who fretted over a dry twig snapping, but he couldn't shake the feeling that something, or someone, was following him.

A seasoned soldier, one matured in the last war of the Horizons, Ornsell wasn't afraid of any man bearing a sword, nor even some who cast magic. Nature was his only concern and by paying his respects to the Great Mother every spring, he didn't have anything to be afraid of. No, no matter how many times he thought about it, still something just wasn't right.

I hope Skann's boys are not in the mood for one of their pranks again or they're going have a day's worth of bottom ache when I finish with them. Those kids smell trouble from afar, especially since their father doesn't give them a good beating when they deserve it. Still, Ornsell went on, despite knowing quite well that a kid's prank would not leave such a vile sense in the back of his mind and that they would not dare venture this far into the forest alone.

Looking around, Ornsell suddenly realized that he had no idea where he was. The sun's bright rays barely crept between the leaves of the mighty evergreen and oak forest. Shadows were dancing as grey clouds passed above the thick forest. Cold sweat started to run down Ornsell's spine.

Whatever is following me can't be good. His left hand instinctively rested on the handle of his axe. Then he slowly pulled it out as his heart pounded fiercely in his chest. His brown eyes quickly examined his surroundings, trying to make out what had made that noise. Unaware of what was chasing him, he decided to follow his instincts and run. His warrior's sense of intuition, honed in the heat of the battle, was the only reason he was still alive after all of these years. The few times he didn't hear them, or he ignored them, he ended up in the back lines, limping and nursing his injuries.

Ornsell saw a break in the forest and took off, crashing through the forest for a full ten minutes, unable to spot anything in the dark behind him. The rustling of the fallen leaves being squashed under his boots became more apparent, and a few cracking twigs that he didn't break sent him jumping behind a large giant oak tree, noticing a terrible pain in his right ankle as he did so. His mind wasn't sure that something was actually following him, but his gut kept shouting a warning. *You have to run, old Orn, you have to run and hide!* With his right ankle aching badly he knew that the only way to get out of there alive was to either hide or fight.

He ran into a clearing amidst the dark woods. Ornsell knew that this place was his best chance for salvation. He was never one for hiding, especially not when he had a perfectly good axe in his right hand and solid ground beneath him. But he knew not to ignore his gut, so he brazenly ran towards the golden light of the still rising sun. Ornsell was sure he could sense the freezing breath of some vile creature on his neck. With desperation, Ornsell dove into the illuminating circle of the glade, landing roughly into a throng of black twigs and unearthed roots.

Gasping, he quickly stood on his feet once again. The warmth of the sun falling on his shoulder was relieving. Hungry for air, he looked around, searching for a good reason to explain his panic. *What is going on inside these woods?*

When he heard the flapping of the wings, it was already too late to do anything about it. The moment the talons of the creature penetrated his shoulders the forest echoed with his pained scream.

Dropping his axe, Ornsell could do nothing but bare the excruciating pain of his whole body being carried aloft by some large feathered monstrosity through the gap in the forest. As they rose he grabbed desperately at the clawed talons, but he could barely move his arms the brutal grip was so tight. HThe talons sunk in even deeper and then he passed out. Moments later, Ornsell regained his senses only to find himself released from the grip of the monster and falling on the outskirts of the forest, close to his home. His steep fall was painful, knocking the wind from him. The flapping stopped with a solid thump on the ground next to him.

"It has been years since the last time I saw humans. You haven't changed a bit, still fragile and puny, like maggots swinging their tails to the sun." A woman's twisted voice boomed behind him. Unable to talk, Ornsell tried to keep up by examining the talking creature. "Oh, you're still conscious. That is commendable. You're lucky that I'm not here to kill you, human, although you'll soon wish I had. I'm here to deliver a curse to you and let the world know that we're back. The legends have come back to life, and soon every nightmare will haunt you whilst you still lie awake without slumber."

Ornsell heard the hoarse voice of the monster mumble in a language unknown to him. His eyes were barely able to focus on the monster's figure; hands full of dark feathers, long feet that ended in sharp talons, pitch black eyes. The legends were true when they spoke of dark creatures that once roamed the land of Theugua. This creature was one of the worst, a harpy witch.

Her feathered hands moved in unison, her words giving a hazy rhythm. The dark magic of those creatures needed no instrument or guidance. Sounds coming from the darkest corners of his mind made a crude melody to accompany them.

Being a Bard in the past, Ornsell knew something of magic. Whatever magic this creature had done to him seemed bad indeed.

She took a step forward and looked over him. With one of her black feathers, she touched the wound in his back. A drop of scarlet blood glistened on the feather when she stepped away. With a sharp pull, she uprooted it from her body and let the droplet run all the way to its root. When the dark red sparkle dropped to the earth, a feeling like fire started spreading from Ornsell's legs and up his back. Cackling like some insane parrot, the harpy witch swiped him across his cheek with a sharp talon then vaulted into the sky, cackling as she flew away into the distance.

His feverish thoughts ran wild. The burning feeling in his legs and back was getting worse with each passing second. Pain usually sharpened his senses, but the throbbing pain just clouded his mind. *I have to get home. I have to. . . ,* but he was unable to complete that thought. His body was stubborn like most people from Midvein, with a strong mind. Blinded by pain and rage, he thought of his family as he crawled towards his home.

Vygarast chortled as he escorted young Noelene to the mansion just outside of Midvein. He was with a beautiful young girl who was pleasant company for him. Noelene was a sweet servant to the local royalty and was destined to live and die under the command of her mistress. But even though her fate was already known, Noelene always shared her sweetest smile with everyone.

The young Bard knew that he would soon complete his training under master Lanarast (that old geezer was always boozing and piping) and that he would soon venture out of Midvein to see the world. However, Noelene was still a great pleasure to be with. The young woman was quick to complain that she imposed on him, but every time they arrived in front of Vygarast's house, she stopped and insisted they stand together to say their goodbye.

"Don't worry sweet Noelene. My father is a grown man and can stand a few hours without my company."

She blushed as Vygarast approached her and put his hand around her shoulders. "But my mistress always sees us together. I can't let her think that something is happening between us. It would dishonor her and Lady Aderfell. I can't do that to her."

Embarrassed, she lowered her eyes and tried to get away from Vygarast's sweet but firm grip. But the young man was charming and his bright green eyes had long cast their net to catch Noelene's heart. "Don't worry. If that ever happens, I will restore your honor by asking your hand in wedding. You know that I'm an honorable man, one who always keeps his word, right?"

The blond girl did not answer. Her eyes were wide open, her hand stretched, pointing towards Vygarast's house.

"What is going on Noelene? Is everything okay?" Before he was able to complete his thought, Vygarast looked towards the house himself.

He strode as fast as he could, almost losing his footing a couple of times along his way, hurrying to his father's motionless body. He was a bloody mess on the ground and Ornsell growled like a wounded animal when Vygarast got to him.

"Father! Father, what's wrong? Father, who did this to you?"

With great pain and with the last of his immense strength, Ornsell whispered in an agonized voice: "...harpy witch..."

Check out the rest of the story in book or audio book format on my website: www.LordHartRules.com

My Other Books and Audio Books

For A Special Treat, check out my
AUDIO BOOKS

Thanks for reading!

If you enjoyed this book a nice review would be greatly appreciated.

Check Out all My Books and Audio Books at:
www.LordHartRules.com